RIPPLES ACROSS THE BAY

RIPPLES ACROSS THE BAY

An anthology of short stories
by
Forthwrite Writer's Group

iUniverse, Inc.
New York Lincoln Shanghai

Ripples Across the Bay

iUniverse books may be ordered through booksellers or by contacting:

iUniverse
2021 Pine Lake Road, Suite 100
Lincoln, NE 68512
www.iuniverse.com
1-800-Authors (1-800-288-4677)

This is a work of fiction. All of the characters, names, incidents, organizations and dialogue in this novel are either the products of the author's imagination or are used fictitiously.

ISBN-13: 978-0-595-40340-0 (pbk)
ISBN-13: 978-0-595-84716-7 (ebk)
ISBN-10: 0-595-40340-9 (pbk)
ISBN-10: 0-595-84716-1 (ebk)

Printed in the United States of America

The Forthwrite Writer's Group

The Forthwrite Writer's Group was formed by three persuasive scribblers. It is now a ten-strong mix of enthusiastic and reluctant writers. Their aim and accomplishment is this book of short stories.

Contents

Introduction

The Forthwrite Writer's Group was formed several years ago in order to provide a forum for people who like to write. It was really a spin off from one of the Readers' Groups organised by Dalgety Bay Library. Dalgety Bay is situated on the Forth Estuary in Fife—hence the reason for the name *Forthwrite*. The group varies considerably in age, background, experience and writing ability, and the reader will soon discover such variation in this volume of short stories. What is held in common within the group is the pleasure in fabricating something interesting with words.

These stories are being published not because they exhibit literary excellence, and certainly not because a profit on book sales is anticipated, but simply because most writers appreciate some kind of feedback in respect of their work. There are several difficulties with publishing these days. One is that it is nearly impossible, at least for anyone who is not already an established author or a celebrity. You send off your story to a short story competition and it is never heard from again. Or you send your novel to innumerable publishing houses and it returns to you increasingly marked by rejection and by the stains of innumerable coffee cups. In the meantime, time passes and passes and passes some more. To many writers, it is beginning to seem that the chief attribute of many "best sellers" is merely the quantity of publisher's hype surrounding the work.

So the members of Forthwrite decided to publish this collection just for the heck of it, and in order to see some of their own work in print and then perhaps receive some feedback which might better their future efforts. Many thanks are due to the staff of Dalgety Bay Library, who provide not merely a meeting room for the group but also encouragement. Particular thanks are due to librarians Brenda Hoyle and Margaret Rhind who kindly arranged to have these stories read and criticised by several anonymous readers. To these critics our gratitude is also expressed. Finally, our thanks must be expressed to the families and friends of group members. They have all contributed in some way to this publication.—*The Editor*

Ripples Across The Bay

By Rosemary Damianos

Braehead used to be just a name on a local map to most people. Nobody out-side Fife, apart from horticulturists and ramblers, had ever heard of the place; which suited the inhabitants of that small town, population 11,572, just fine. It sits on the Forth estuary and on a clear day, Edinburgh is plainly visible across the river. The town itself is surrounded by fertile farmland and prides itself on the skill of its gardeners and its success in local and national horticultural com-petitions. This was also its undoing.

Now that the journalists and their satellite vans have decamped and we can claim our town again, it was decided that the record ought to be set straight. To make the account as clear as possible, the main participants have agreed to put their testimonies on record.

Perhaps it would be as well to introduce them.

Margery Kirkstone-Hall is the President of Braehead Horticultural Society, and has been so for the past 45 years. Her family owned much of the surround-ing land before the war; but as with so many families in their position, post-war conditions forced the sale of their estate and she now lives in the old dower house surrounded by modern houses.

Margaret Hope is the society's secretary and has been in post almost as long as her old friend Margery. They attended the same school and served together during the war as FANY's.

The Reverend Walter Scott became the incumbent of the new church after the tragic loss of the elderly minister in a mysterious blaze that destroyed the old church five years ago. Many people still regret his passing, and view the modern brick building with considerable disfavour. The Reverend Walter Scott is not looked upon with favour either and is treated with dour Christian for-bearance by his congregation.

Andrew Carmichael is a recluse and occasionally appears to recite his poetry at literary festivals, when not busy up at his allotment. He used to be the church organist but left in disgust when the church authorities replaced it with a synthesizer. Anonymous letters appeared in the local press about the godlessness of the minister and church, after the minister formed a gospel rock group and played his electric guitar at an evening service.

Margery

I was putting the final touches to the judges' roster for the annual show. It was made particularly difficult this year, because two of our judges had muddled their diaries and had double booked themselves for the Kelty show as well. Really, you would think they would have more sense. I wouldn't be at all surprised if they weren't getting past it. Still, silver clouds and all that. I managed to get Colm and Bunty Weston! That was quite a coup, I can tell you. They were judging at Chelsea this year. Where was I? Oh yes, fixing the roster wasn't I?

I had just printed out the list when the doorbell and telephone rang. Naturally I attended to the telephone and let my cleaning woman see to the door. The phone call wasn't that interesting, just some blighter trying to sell me some double glazing or life insurance or something. Couldn't really tell, I'd forgotten to turn on my hearing aid. No matter. My visitor was unexpected and I showed him into the kitchen. It took a cup of coffee and *three* chocolate biscuits before he could tell me what the problem was. Well, as soon as I'd got hold of the right end of the stick, I donned my gumboots and drove us up to the allotment.

To be quite candid, I thought Andrew was drunk. I mean to say, one does not expect to come across bodies in one's brassicas. But blow me, there it was. Stiff as a board. I bent to check, and it seemed as if it had been deep frozen. I could understand Andrew's wrath, a whole year's work flattened and of course I tried to buck him up. Then it struck us! The judges were due to visit the allotments the following afternoon. We moved away and stood by the shed. If we called the police, they'd put the place out of bounds and we'd be out of the competition. Well there was only one thing to be done, of course. We'd have to remove the chap until the judges had been. The thing is, neither of us could think where to park him. I'm a great believer in working out problems by a spot of hard work, so we went to borrow Ada's trolley so that we could get the chap out of the bed and try to repair the damage if we could. I really must speak to Ada about that trolley of hers, and get her to return it to the garden centre.

The brassicas were done for I'm afraid, so I left Andrew digging them up. He must have lost his clothes, the chap was naked apart from a bit of sacking. Young and a bit scrawny, definitely not a local lad. He was grey, and as I said, frozen solid. Thought I'd better get hold of Margaret and have a council of war, so Andrew put the chap in the shed and stood guard until I got back.

Margaret

I was in the garden doing a bit of weeding, before selecting my flowers for the show. I had just reached the compost bin when I heard Margery crunch up the path. Her hair was all over the place and her face seemed ruddier than usual. Usually when she comes visiting, she tidies herself up a bit. I waved and finished tipping the contents of my bucket into the bin.

We went to sit in the shade and I brought out some lemonade while Margery tidied herself up a bit. She's never beaten about the bush, well we learned not to, and told me about the chap in the allotment. I must say, it was really rotten luck for Andrew. I mean to say, the patch next door has been empty for ages since Willie Millar went to live with his sister in Spain. Just a few feet would have made all the difference. I suppose it means that Gavin Brown will get best in show again. Poor Andrew, he really had such a good chance this year to finally lift that trophy.

Margery lit a cigarette and scowled at my new bed. I know we've been friends since we were six, but even friendship has its limits and I was not going to dig it up again, now that the plants had finally established themselves and we couldn't put him in the church; that was being used for the show, and exhibitors were already tripping over each other, and we racked our brains for a safe place. It's surprising what pops back into your memory. We both said *Jacques* and memories of Poitiers surfaced. It could work, but we'd need some help. Honestly, what a thing to happen just before the show. Margery and I then went back over to the allotments, after calling in to see the minister.

Andrew

Whit's the point of it aw? Whit's the bloody point? Some glaikit article couldnae dae his job and…ach whit's the point?

Better write this down in proper English, but ma hert's nae in it.

I got up to the place at the back of seven. Rab was already there but he's as deaf as a post and didn't see me. I saw that something was wrong when I passed

Ada's shed. I saw some silly bugger sleeping in my brassicas. Man I was ready to kill him, but he was already deid. I've seen bodies before, but this was something else. He was stiff and grey and didnae have a stitch on. I covered him wi' a bit of sacking from the shed and went to get Mrs Kirkstone-Hall. Ah hadnae touched him and didnae want any trouble. She's no a bad soul, her bark's worse than her bite and she has a good heid on her.

When she came, we put him in the shed and I tidied up my row after she had gone. Ada arrived and started gieing me laldy when she couldn't find her trolley. I told her that someone must have taken it back to where it came from. That made me feel a bit better, seeing her all upset and knowing that it was in my shed.

Mrs Kirkstone-Hall sent her over to the church to help, when she came back with Mrs Hope. They went into the shed and came out again and walked up and down having a good blether. Then they asked me to go and get a sheet. When I got back, they had gone. So had the body. I never saw it again.

The Reverend Walter Scott

I was working on the Parish magazine when my wife Marigold told me that I had two visitors. I could see from her agitation that they were important and I wondered who they were. I heard them as I crossed the hall from my study and I have to confess that my heart sank. Mrs Hope is convenor of the church flower committee and puts the wind up me. Mrs Kirkstone-Hall is what I can only describe as a force to be reckoned with. My heart sank even further when they turned their smiles on me. The last time they had done so, I found myself abseiling off the Forth Bridge and it was an experience that I shall never ever repeat, even if the church was falling down about my ears and the elders were facing bankruptcy.

They came to the point at once and of course I insisted that the police were summoned without delay. They turned their hyena smiles on me again and explained that that would not be convenient, given the show and the judging schedule. I should have stood up to them, but my will was weak and I agreed to help them against my better judgement. I hope that will be taken in mitigation, especially as I refused to allow church property to be used.

They took me to see the unfortunate soul. He really was frozen solid and I didn't recognize him, even though I'm involved with several youth groups. I admit that I was intrigued by him and by his manner of arrival. Of course, he couldn't stay where he was and I made the call to my brother-in-law. He was not told the truth and is totally innocent in this matter; I must insist that that is put on the record. He is an undertaker and agreed to hold the body for a day or two.

The incident would probably have escaped notice but for an unfortunate series of events, beginning with the discovery of some false teeth.

'Sarge, you're having me on. False teeth? Someone handed in a set of false teeth?'

'Not one set laddie, a whole bagful of false teeth. I want you to go round to see Mrs McMurray, here's her address. Try and find out all you can. She's missing a few biscuits from the barrel if you get my drift, so go easy on her.'

'OK Sarge. What happened to Alison?'

'She took Mrs McMurray home, but she radioed that the old lady preferred to talk to a real policeman, not a little girl.'

PC Hatton grinned and winked at Detective Sergeant Henderson and saw her face redden as he left the station. He never arrived. Taking a shortcut through Meadow Woods, he stumbled over a low lying branch and found himself looking into the eyes of a very stiff and very dead body. He staggered away from the scene and brought up his lunch of pork pie, beans, chips, jam sponge and custard. When he finished retching, he radioed for back up and waited for his colleagues.

'Good god, this chappie is frozen solid! Impossible to give you a time of death until we thaw him out. Where on earth did he come from I wonder?'

'Could he have been brought here, Doc?'

'Highly unlikely. See? It looks like he dropped like a stone, there's no obvious tracks around and you certainly couldn't have brought a vehicle in without leaving any evidence. No footprints either apart from the Constable's. I'll take a look at him when I'm finished here. He looks a bit the worse for wear.'

'Let's go through it one more time. You were on your way to see a Mrs. McMurray in Appin Way. That's right? And you decided to go through the woods?'

'Yes sir. It's a short cut. My partner was already there in the squad car, so I walked. It's only a 10 minute walk from the station, if you come this way.'

'What happened exactly? Take your time.'

'I thought I heard something so I went to have a look. We've been having some trouble with a group of kids messing around near the old shelter. I tripped over a branch and almost landed on top of him. His eyes were open and it scared the shite out of me. I wasn't expecting to find a frozen corpse.'

'No, I don't suppose you were Constable. What did you hear? Do you think there was anyone else nearby?'

'I don't think so sir. There are a lot of squirrels in these woods. I had a look round afterwards, but I didn't see anything. I kept away from the crime scene.'

'OK. The Doc will have a look at you. After that, you'd better get back to the station to write up your report. Someone else can go to Mrs McMurray.'

'Yes sir.'

They had to carry the body to the path and as they lifted it, a small rubber pouch fell out of his shirt. The doctor bent and carefully picked it up with his pen and slid it into a plastic bag, before handing it over.

Back at the station, Jimmy Hatton was having his leg mercilessly pulled. Not only was he new to the force, he was from Glasgow, where bodies were supposed to be commonplace. The joking stopped abruptly when the Sergeant appeared.

'Hatton, the Inspector wants to see you. The rest of you, get back to work.'

'Sit down Jimmy. Are you feeling better? Is this your first time? Well, I can't say you ever get used to it, but your stomach might. Now, this case is to be kept under wraps for the time being. Special Branch is going to investigate it. It seems that our friend is of interest to them. So no talking. When your report is ready, I want to see it.'

'Yes sir.

'Very good, carry on.'

'Thank you sir.'

The annual show seemed to be more popular than ever, and Margery beamed as she welcomed the judges and introduced them to the stewards who would be accompanying them. The exhibits filled the hall and the side rooms and nervous competitors clustered round the tea urn, waiting for the verdict.

Margaret sighed with pleasure as she gazed at the *Best in Show* card sitting squarely in front of her magnificent fuchsias and tried to hide her girlish delight at her haul of rosettes. Margery was tight-lipped when she came second to Eleanor Moody in the marmalade section, but remembered her manners sufficiently to offer her congratulations.

Margery found herself having to deal with less well mannered competitors and stepped in to stop a fist fight between two rival leek growers. She watched the judges depart with enormous relief, delighted that they had been enjoying lavish hospitality in the judges' room at the time and had not witnessed the melee in the main hall.

'I think it all went splendidly, Margaret. Robin told me that the allotment judges didn't seem to notice anything amiss. I spoke to Andrew earlier, he's still very upset about yesterday of course, but I think he's calming down.

Have you seen the minister? He seems to have wandered off. I told him I wanted to have a little word after the judges left. Do you think you could see if he's hiding anywhere? I need to talk to June about the WRI display. See you later for a sherry?'

Margery

Just as I was about to leave the church car park, I found my way barred by two scruffy looking hoodlums. Naturally I asked them to remove themselves not only from the vicinity of my car but also from the car park. When they declined to oblige, I told them I was a Magistrate and would ensure that they did so. Then I saw that snivelling little man and his dreary wife, who was making a public spectacle of herself with all that *quite* unnecessary wailing, and they told me I was under arrest! I thought that was a joke in extremely poor taste but when they showed me their warrant cards, I realised that it wasn't. They put the minister in one car and me in the other.

They tried to interrogate me, but compared to the Gestapo, they were hopelessly out of their depth. I remained silent until my solicitor sat down beside me and then I answered their questions. Then they had to let me go. I passed Mrs Scott and discovered that her husband had been remanded in custody for further questioning. I'm not at all surprised; and she took my well meant advice very badly indeed.

Margaret

I couldn't understand what had kept Margery. She is normally very punctual. It was only when I got home and heard her message, I found out what had happened. Well naturally, I immediately got in touch with our solicitor. We've both used the same firm for over half a century, although it's the grandson we deal with now. I passed on Margery's message and waited by the phone.

It was such a relief to see her shadow at my front door. I gave her a stiff drink and we decided to go for a walk in the garden. Just as well really. I didn't notice anything amiss until I was getting ready for bed. I noticed that the table underneath my phone was very clean indeed. And then I noticed that one or two ornaments were not quite as I had left them. I had a spring clean in the morning and found rather too many bugs for my liking.

When I met Margery at the Post Office I told her that she ought to check her house too, only to discover that she had already done so. I must say, it's all getting a little exciting. I hope we're doing the right thing.

The Reverend Walter Scott

I've been away on a retreat. I'm still having trouble sleeping and Marigold has decided to stay with her sister in Wales. I like police dramas on television, especially *Morse*, but I don't really think that I'll watch any more. It would be too harrowing.

I was working in my vestry, well hiding from Mrs Kirkstone-Hall, when these two louts burst in. I thought they were intent on robbing me and I reached for my phone. I don't know what happened exactly, I found myself pinned to the floor with my arms being twisted up behind my back. They were very rough and it wasn't until they dragged me outside that I heard one of them gabbling about my right to remain silent. Marigold tried to come to my rescue and they were going to arrest her too, but then let her go when Mrs Kirkstone-Hall appeared. They didn't seem to frighten her at all and they showed her their warrant cards. Then I knew they really were policemen and not kidnappers.

Marigold told me, when they finally let me see her, that Mrs Kirkstone-Hall had been released and had left with a solicitor. It didn't occur to either of us that one might be needed. I was finally released on police bail, after Marigold brought in my passport and a letter from my superiors. They suggested I go on retreat and I couldn't refuse. The days are very dark indeed. My poor innocent brother-in-law was visited by the police and only the skill of his solicitor kept him out of their clutches too.

'Hatton!'

'Yes Sarge. Coming Sarge.'

'I want you and Young to go and bring Andrew Carmichael in for a little chat. He'll probably be up at the allotments, so try there first. If not, you'll find him at his cottage on the Braefoot Road. It's the last one, you can't miss it. The garden is a real treat.'

'Right oh. We're on our way.'

After you've stopped off for doughnuts probably, muttered Sergeant King. The station was bursting at the seams and nobody was supposed to notice the presence of the SB. The local force was resentful to a man at the way they had been sidelined by them and the way their mess had been commandeered and was now off-limits. The allotments seemed deserted and they were about to go back to their car when Ada's high pitched scream brought them running. Her eyes were wide and her mouth was working furiously, but no sound came out.

They looked over to where she pointed her hoe and saw a Hessian bundle on a trolley.

'Stay with her, Joe. I'll go and see what's going on.'

PC Hatton sounded a lot braver than he felt and he walked towards the trolley. He used his truncheon to move the sacking and found a bundle of wood and some tools. He grinned and turned to summon his colleague when a movement caught the corner of his eye. Joe Young just managed to catch him before his head struck the corner of the wall.

They covered their noses as the stench wafted towards them and hastily turned away. PC Young called on his radio and once more his colleagues gathered to view another body.

'Who is it, laddie? Do we know?'

'Yes Doc. Andrew Carmichael. He's our local bard and gives poetry readings. I've never heard any of them, mind.'

'I see. Well he won't be giving any more readings. At a rough estimate, I'd say he's been dead about a week at most. Hello…what's this?' The doctor dangled a rubber pouch at the end of his pen. 'I've seen this before. It looks like the one I found on the frozen chap. Better bag it. This is a hopeless mess. I can't say how long this chap has been here, he may not even have died here. Just look at all those footprints. I'll get the results to you as soon as I can, probably towards the middle of next week for the preliminary ones. Who found the body? Not the same chap? Poor blighter!'

The Sergeant nodded.

'Aye. You'd better have a look at both of them after you've finished. The local GP is looking after Ada. Poor soul found him you know.'

'Sarge?'

'Present and correct. What's the news?'

'They've found another frozen body.'

'What?? Are you winding me up?'

'No Sarge. They found him half an hour ago. At the back of Carmichael's cottage.'

'Well, at least Hatton didn't find this one. Poor sod is right off his food. Look, while your boys are out on crow patrol this weekend, do me a favour and keep your eyes open. God knows how many more bodies are waiting out there.'

'Yes Sarge. The boss asked me to find you.'

'OK. Ask Henderson to take over.'

'Sir, you wanted to see me?'

'Yes, come in and close the door. The investigation has been passed back to us. I don't know why, and I've been told to forget that we saw our visitors. The pm on the first frozen body has come back and I've passed the file over to DI Craig. What do you make of all this Bert? You've been tending this patch for 20 years.'

'I've never seen anything like it. I was watching an American police documentary on Reality TV the other night and they showed how illegal immigrants stowed away on aircraft. Perhaps that's how they got here. Maybe they stowed away and when the landing gear went down, they fell out. It was very windy last week and I heard a couple of planes fly over.'

'That's what the doc thought. The frozen chap had died of hypothermia and lack of oxygen. We still don't know where they came from, but the rubber pouches tell an interesting tale. They had diamonds embedded inside. The forensics boys are having a field day. Glad it's their baby and not ours.'

'Is this why you wanted to see me sir?'

'No Bert. More teeth have turned up. Mrs McMurray brought in another bagful and says she found them. Yes I know what you're thinking, but I'd like you to find out what's going on. Do you think Hatton can handle this? Ask him to do it in plain clothes, talk to the neighbours first.'

'Right you are. I'll brief him when he comes on duty. He should be able to get his teeth into this one!'

'Out man! That's your worst pun since the Christmas party.'

The Deputy Chief Constable read the report and called for a strong black coffee. Any hopes of keeping the lid on the trouble at Braehead had now gone out the window. Special Branch had managed to score a spectacular own goal and somebody had leaked it to the press. Frozen bodies were bad enough, but illegal bugging of prominent citizens was quite another, especially if one of the parties was a kinswoman of the Lord Lieutenant and the other a serving magistrate. The press were having a feeding frenzy over that one.

'Get me McBride. We'll need to put out a statement. Have you managed to get in touch with the ladies? Oh good. They suggested meeting in St Andrews? Fine. What? Golf clubs? Oh dear, well I suppose….oh, I see. Is he free? Yes, put it in the diary.'

Margery and Margaret

'More tea Margery?'

'Thank you dear. I paid a call on the new minister this afternoon. He's much more suitable. What a stroke of luck for the committee to find him! I must write a note to the Presbytery Clerk. Not married though. He told me that he wants to put in an organ and knows a very talented organist. It will mean more fundraising again of course. He told me that they'd like to put up a plaque to Andrew when the organ is dedicated. Such a nice gesture, don't you think?'

'Yes indeed. I've heard that there is to be a posthumous edition of his poems. I've never liked them of course; I prefer my poetry to be more lyrical and not so angry. I do hope he didn't mind. But really, it was the only solution.'

'Yes, but I'm sorry that Ada had to find him. She won't be coming back. Matron told me that she had lost all touch with reality and would have to stay in a secure ward. Who's next on the list?'

'Mary and George Peacock and Gladys May. Can't put them near each other, not after that business with the leeks. We'll have to drop one of them down the list and I think we should let that nice young policeman have Willie Millar's.'

'What a good idea! The Peacocks can wait; they're such a pushy couple. They've only been here for five minutes and already they're on every committee but ours. Oh by the way, I heard a most extraordinary story today. I heard it from Jean. You know her sister lives in Appin Way? Yes you do, Margery! Next door to Jessie McMurray. Well, Jessie has managed to get herself into a bit of a pickle. You remember she used to work up at the hospital in the café? She went to the police and told them she'd found some teeth. Yes dear I know, but they took it seriously. Young PC Hatton went undercover and discovered that she'd been helping herself to other people's property, including their teeth! Can you imagine? Everyone's in a right state, Jean said that she'd collected dozens of dentures and the dentist has had to try and sort it all out! Poor Jessie, oh dear! Perhaps I shouldn't have mentioned it to you if she's likely to come before you.'

'That's all right. After chatting to the Chief Constable I've decided to step down. It seemed to be a wise decision after all the fuss. Better to quit while you're ahead, isn't that what the dear old squadron leader used to say?'

'I haven't thought of him for years. I wonder what happened to him? Guy Pendleton wasn't his real name of course; I wonder what it was? Perhaps you're right, dear. We are getting a little long in the tooth to be making waves, but we can still make a ripple or two! How about a *hot lady*? I can still remember Guy's recipe.'

A Swinging Christmas

By William Armstrong

I guess it was bound to happen one day. The pressures of modern society get to everybody sooner or later. At least, so my father said. He was full of those sort of sayings, my old parent. I remember him telling me once when we were making our yearly migration down through the Yukon, with the wolves closing in, just waiting to pick off an unwary straggler: 'Son, some things, like death and migration, never change. You just can't buck the odds.'

So it was a hell of a shock to all the deer and antelope species when Santa's sleigh team went on strike. You see, this was something fundamental. It struck at the very core of everything we had absorbed with our mothers' milk. For centuries we'd been brought up to believe that we were the chosen ones, with some sort of divine right to haul the old gentleman in his sleigh. Sure, it had always been the preserve of the reindeer and they never let us forget it, but some of the glory sorta rubbed off on other members of the family, especially us caribou. After all, we look pretty much like reindeer.

In my opinion it should never have got to a strike, but with the benefit of hindsight it's easy to say that now. There were faults on both sides. Dancer was always a hothead and he tried to force through too many changes too quickly. He wanted some routes re-scheduled, compulsory meal breaks, time off for the rut, sick pay, plus a tonnage bonus and an inclement weather allowance! Oh yes, and a reserve team!

Sadly, S. Claus wasn't the most enlightened of employers when it came to labour relations. His was the autocratic approach. 'Just do as I say. I know what's best.' That's no way to run a transport firm. Unfortunately, faced with Dancer's demands he became obdurate and refused to concede anything.

Attitudes hardened. Comet and Cupid, who had been kinda dubious about the whole thing, now swung solidly behind Dancer. That individual, showing talents few of us thought he possessed, succeeded in bringing all the reindeer in Lapland out in sympathy.

Personally, I reckon Dancer had a point. I know that being part of Santa's team gives you tremendous prestige in the community, but, at the end of the day, you can't eat prestige. At least, that's the way the younger generation saw it. No, the old man should have seen the light years ago.

The trouble really came to a head the previous Christmas. A record tonnage and a series of blizzards had put the team in an ugly mood and they were ripe for rebellion. Dancer saw his chance and confronted the old man with his demands. Even then it might not have been too late, but Santa had twisted his ankle getting down from a particularly high roof, and he was also feeling the strain. Flying into a rage he ordered Dancer out and that was it.

So there we were, with negotiations at an impasse and nobody prepared to give an inch. Of course, it wasn't very long before the word got around. The birds saw to that. Reactions varied. Scandinavia was solid to a deer, if you'll pardon me borrowing a human expression! Elsewhere things were a bit different. The older element kept on about established traditions and the deeply religious significance of Christmas. They felt this was a major crisis and that we would be letting the side down if we didn't muster a team from somewhere.

That went down like a lead balloon with the younger generation. In their view man had done nothing for us since the beginning of time and, if his snot-nosed brats never got any presents that was fine by them.

The argument might have gone on forever if certain other species hadn't decided to take a hand. Up in our neck of the woods the wolves let it be known they were thinking of tendering for the job. For years they had been saddled with this Little Red Riding Hood and Three Little Pigs nonsense and now, at last, here was a golden opportunity to improve their image. Well, that was the gist of their argument anyway.

When it was pointed out, sorta cautiously, that they had no previous experience, their leading spokeswolf bared his fangs and said 'No problem. Our cousins, the huskies, run the Iditarod Trail every year and I'm sure they wouldn't mind showing us the ropes.' After seeing that display of ivory I was certain they wouldn't!

Then the bison tried to horn in. Their view was that they had both the weight and the muscle for the job. After all, oxen hauled wagons didn't they? A sleigh couldn't be that much different. Relations got a bit strained when a skunk, who had no business being there in the first place but nobody felt like telling him, said, 'Fine, if you want the place smelling like a farmyard!' That meeting broke up in disorder and was never reconvened. The bison went off in the huff and that was that.

The only other offer of note, which came from Africa via migratory curlews and the ubiquitous seagulls, was from the elephants. They pointed out that their ancestors had crossed the Alps with Hannibal and who needed a sleigh anyway?

At that point the older members of all the deer and antelope families decided things had gone far enough and convened a series of meetings (six in all) throughout the world. Europe, Asia, Africa, Australia and the two Americas. Antarctica, for Australia declined. Any of our species which were there had been brought by man, and they were quite happy to leave matters to their home countries. Besides, kangaroos just weren't suitable.

It was generally felt that the llamas and associated species, hailing from South America, were borderline cases, but courtesy dictated that they be given the chance to air their views. We should have known better! Their reply, passed on with relish by a condor who had brought it all the way, was most offensive and ended by saying that they wanted nothing to do with such a harebrained scheme. But then, they always were supercilious SOB's anyway!

So we were left with just four meetings. Europe, Asia, Africa and North America. Each indigenous species was invited to send a delegate.

It was only after general agreement had been reached regarding the venues for these meetings, that it dawned on everybody just how difficult it would be for the delegates to get there unscathed. Even if it wasn't the hunting season, few men would be able to resist taking a potshot at a prime elk, or moose, traipsing across their land. And on top of that there were our natural predators, such as wolves, cougars and bears. In Africa it was even worse. Lions, leopards, hyenas and hunting dogs, plus, as the gnus pointed out, the odd crocodile thrown in! Asia, although it wasn't quite so bad, still posed problems. Not on the same scale of course, carnivores are a bit more localised there, but the delegates from India would still need help, at least until they were clear of the sub-continent. Their meeting was being held in central China.

Preparations for the European meeting collapsed when the delegates said they would not cross a picket line set up by Dancer and his teammates.

So there we were, down to just three meetings. At that point there was a lot of muttering behind the scenes about the whole thing being a complete waste of time. In the end however, the majority view prevailed and we moved on to the next stage in the plan, negotiating safe passage for the delegates. All this, as you can imagine, involved a great deal of long distance communication, and here I must pay tribute to the birds for their efforts in carrying information to and from the various meetings. I could understand the enthusiasm of the doves for instance. After all, Christmas is part and parcel of their background as well. However, the seagulls really surprised all of us. They put in hours and hours of extra flying time.

Finally, all the rules for safe passage were more or less agreed and the dates of the meetings were set. I say more or less because, while most of the carnivores were quite reasonable, there were individuals who either couldn't be contacted, or else flatly refused to co-operate. This meant laying on escorts from further afield through the danger zones, which tested species relationships severely. The first mule deer delegate, heading north from Wyoming, was ambushed and killed by a cougar, up in the high country. There was, as you can imagine, a hell of an outcry. The cats apologised profusely, but it was felt that their explanation about a scattered population and the difficulty in controlling splinter groups, was somewhat thin, to say the least. However, some good did come out of the unfortunate incident. The deceased had come from Yellowstone National Park and the park's grizzlies took exception. They seemed to feel their honour had been impugned, or something like that. Anyway, they issued a statement saying they would personally guarantee the safety of any delegate under their protection! The elk representative, coming from Colorado, took them up on their offer and headed for Yellowstone. On the way he picked up the mule deer replacement, a good-looking lady and one of the few female delegates.

They were met at the park boundary by two giant silvertip grizzlies, who proceeded to run interference for them all the way to the meeting place on Peace River. What with the female company and the novelty of the whole situation, the elk was on a high when he got there. He reckoned their journey through Yellowstone had done wonders for the tourist trade!

Their escort turned back a few miles south of the meeting place and the farewells must have been quite something! 'You know,' the elk said pensively, 'I felt real sad seein' them big fellas disappearin' down the trail. Don't reckon I'll ever sleep as sound again. Still, when I get back I guess I'll be able to pull any female with my story!'

Whether the bison got wind of this or not we never found out, but they buried the hatchet and brought the moose delegate up in one of their herds. I spoke to him afterwards and he said while the journey was all right, it was also very boring. 'Let's face it,' he said, 'if you've seen one bison you've seen 'em all.'

Elsewhere things went pretty well, although there was one tragic incident in Africa which highlighted just how close to the wind we were sailing The sable antelope delegate was crossing the Ngorongoro crater with a lion escort, when it happened. Now, I have to tell you that sable antelope are tough dudes and quick on the trigger. They may respect lions, but by and large they don't fear them, and this bull was no exception.

One of the escort, a big black-maned male, remarked that he was partial to antelope meat, whereupon the sable said 'Oh yeah, you and whose army!' or words to that effect and promptly head-butted the cat. Bearing in mind that the head in question was equipped with twin, three foot long, needle sharp horns, the lion never really knew what hit him. The other half of the escort piled in, and when the dust settled there was one very dead lion and an equally defunct sable antelope. Oh yes, and according to a vulture who was first on the scene, and was later called to give evidence, the surviving cat didn't look too good either!

Well, that created a real foul up. The lions, supported by the leopards, withdrew all further co-operation and it looked as though we'd come to the end of the trail. However, and for this magnanimous gesture we, the deer and antelope family will be forever in their debt; the elephants and buffalo agreed to escort all the remaining African delegates waiting to get through. The gnus, wildebeest and impala were delighted with the arrangement. The only real objection came, as usual, from the sable antelope. They felt there was a principle at stake. Their replacement made an impassioned speech to a gathering of herbivores, in which he said it was a free continent and he'd go where he damned well pleased.

A massacre was only prevented by the intervention of a bull elephant from the Aberdare National Park, who took the recalcitrant delegate aside and explained, very patiently, that he was going to the meeting under escort, whether he liked it or not. Mind you, the sable only saw the light when the tusker uprooted a sapling which he proceeded to wave around to emphasise his remarks. At that point the delegate decided, grudgingly, 'that well, yes, he might just be prepared to go along.'

Of course there was a fair bit of snarling and swearing from the carnivores, but it all died away when the elephants pointed out, mildly, that they had never previously leaned on anyone, but if they had to…. Whereupon the lions and their allies left hurriedly. The hyenas tried to make a joke about the whole affair, but when the rhinos asked them what the hell they were laughing at they too moved off pretty quickly.

So, after what seemed an interminable delay, the three remaining meetings finally got under way. There were speeches from all the delegates, each making a case for the inclusion of one of their species in the team. I don't know what it was like elsewhere, but exchanges became quite heated at the Peace River convention. It had already been agreed that votes would decide the places and a great deal of intensive lobbying went on behind the scenes. Eventually however, all the votes were cast and counted, and the team took shape. It was a strange mixture. Each meeting had been allowed to put forward two candidates. At Peace River we voted for the caribou and the elk. There was some surprise that the moose hadn't done better, but their delegate didn't come across at all well. I suppose it was understandable really. They tend to be loners.

Asia went for the sambar and the sika, pretty much as expected.

Africa was the problem. To everybody's embarrassment the wildebeest topped the poll! Well, I mean…they're not the best advert for herbivores. The eland came second. That was a turn-up! There had been a lot of muttering that they were distantly related to cattle. However, their delegate gave a long reasoned dissertation on eland history, pointing out that this story had been concocted by man and was a scurrilous attack on the good name of elands everywhere. Obviously the sympathy vote had been a big factor.

The remaining two places were, in effect, wild cards. They went to the sable antelope and the moose, with the nilgai as a standby reserve.

Of course, all this movement of wild life by land and air hadn't gone unnoticed by man. According to the seagulls, who used to check on any old newspapers they found when scavenging the rubbish dumps, all sorts of theories were being put forward. It was global warming. It was the long-term effects of radiation. And so on. Naturalists had noted that certain species, normally hunters and hunted, had been seen apparently co-operating and this worried the humans considerably. The gulls said there were dark mutterings about this having been foretold and the names of certain humans, notably Hitchcock and Orwell, were being bandied about at length. One eminent church leader spoke about the 'new dawn' and the 'lion and the lamb lying down together!' This report was relayed to the bighorn sheep, whereupon one old ram remarked sourly that, 'he didn't know nothin' 'bout lions, but he sure as hell weren't lyin' down with no cougar!'

Anyway, there we were with eight 'good men and true,' if you'll pardon the expression. All we needed now was Santa's approval, which he duly gave and we were in business. It was agreed that there should be a number of trial runs to let the team shake down so to speak, and when you considered the diversity of the species involved you could see why.

Don't imagine Dancer and his chums hadn't realised what was happening. The reindeer pickets were out in force and the team had them really fired up. Rudolph had been hitting the bottle pretty heavily and he was shooting his mouth off to anyone who would listen. Drink's always been his problem. He didn't get that nose from mineral water! Still, I don't think anyone was too bothered about his wild threats.

Donner and Blitzen now...they were different. 'Ve haff vays of preventing your team from getting through.' And I've no doubt they had. I think it was at this point Dancer began to see that the goodwill which the team had built up over the years was rapidly being eroded. He hurriedly convened a meeting of the strikers and proposed that, as a gesture of conciliation and Christmas spirit, the replacements should be allowed to cross the picket line. I gather things became very heated and all sorts of accusations were bandied about. Suffice to say the issue went to a vote and was carried five-three. Long afterwards I heard that Dancer had made sure of Prancer, Vixen, Comet and Cupid's votes, before the meeting began.

The matter of getting the team together was left in Santa's hands and I regret I'm not allowed to divulge how he did it. There were all sorts of paranormal and psychic stories circulating of course, but when I questioned Pa, who was on the Inner Council, he muttered darkly about not prying into things I wouldn't understand.

The first two practise runs were done in the temperate zones, just to get everyone 'bedded in' as it were.

Overall things went pretty well, although the wildebeest did cause problems by shying at imaginary dangers. However, a sharp dig in the ribs from the sable put an end to that nonsense.

Then, just when everything in the garden seemed lovely, Santa fell and broke his leg! A bad fracture it was too. There were expressions of sympathy from the strikers, but the fact that the old gentleman tripped over an empty bucket, which just happened to be lying outside the loading bay doors, gave everyone considerable food for thought.

All three meetings were hurriedly reconvened and the consensus of opinion was that we were up the proverbial creek, sans paddle! Of course there were lots of 'I told you so' remarks behind the scenes, and I must say the outlook seemed pretty bleak. But, as the humans say, 'cometh the hour, cometh the man', or in this case the sable antelope delegate. In an impassioned address to the African meeting he said he was damned if anyone was going to laugh at the herbivores while he was around. His revolutionary proposal was that we should find a stand-in for Santa. Such a replacement, he maintained, could only come from one group, the apes!

The bird messengers worked shifts passing information between the meetings and, after the initial shock, it was agreed that we had no other choice. Accordingly, the chimpanzees, gorillas and orang-utans were contacted and sounded out on the idea.

As it turned out there was no contest. Both larger ape species declined and the chimpanzee was nominated unopposed. Our meeting tried to drum up some interest in a bigfoot nominee, but, as they couldn't be contacted in time the idea was dropped. Asia abandoned the idea of a yeti candidate for the same reason.

The African meeting asked for candidates to come forward, and about twenty chimpanzees from all over the continent turned up.

Of course you must realise that all this was relayed to us third or fourth hand, and each time the story got a little amended in the telling. Anyway, from what we heard, it appeared that a good two thirds of the chimps were real hicks from the sticks and hadn't a clue about what they were taking on. Of the remainder, one candidate, a chimpanzee called Ngaro, from down on the East African coast, was, by all accounts, a sensation. Well groomed, quietly spoken, and with all the right answers, he was a shoo-in! It further transpired that he was a rehabilitated individual who had spent his formative years on film sets in Hollywood. His return to the wild had been engendered by one of those periodic attacks of conscience which humans are prone to. Now, his one aim, or so he said, was to help make this a better world for everyone. After that peroration there was never any doubt that here was our replacement.

Santa bitched about the whole idea, but when it was pointed out that he either agreed or else cancelled Christmas, S. Claus gave in. In fact, once he met Ngaro the old gentleman became quite co-operative. He gave the chimp a crash course in packaging and distribution, and just stopped short of adding climbing to the curriculum!

So the trial runs began, and went very well. Ngaro was politeness itself where the team was concerned, though they later admitted that his free and easy ways; 'just call me Randy,' and 'waggons roll,' or 'let's boogie,' when he wanted them to move on was somewhat disconcerting. Also, his favourite catchphrase, 'let's make it a swinging Christmas,' did not please everyone. Still, as the elk, something of a swinger himself said, 'the world is a-changin' and we just gotta move with the times.' Even now I wake up at night sweating when I think what the outcome might have been!

Came the big night and Ngaro and the team got down to business. It was a typical Christmas Eve, with just the right amount of frost and snow. Everything went well, or so the team said when they reported back. Even Santa admitted that they seemed not to have done too badly.

Then the complaints started coming in. There appeared to have been a spate of burglaries along the team's routes and the police were at a loss to explain them. In every case the thief, or thieves, had made off with jewellery. Also, large numbers of irate parents reported that their offspring had found some very explicit pornographic literature and small packets of a white substance in their stockings!

Just about this time Ngaro made some excuse about taking a sabbatical to recover and that was the last anyone saw of him.

That's when just about everything hit the fan. I'll draw a veil over what followed. Suffice to say Santa and his team took a lot of stick, unfairly in my opinion. Still, the resultant hoo-ha did some good. Dancer and Co. modified their demands, and Santa undertook to implement a more liberal regime.

And Ngaro, or Randy if you prefer? Disappeared completely. Mind you, there have been persistent rumours about a band of chimpanzees near the headwaters of the Congo, who, so the story goes, not only wear jewellery but have succumbed to most of the vices known to man. Well, after all, what else could you expect from a coke sniffing, light-fingered, rehabilitated ape who used to star in porno movies!

The Snakeskin Shoes

By Maureen Brister

Lizzie Pasterman (Anderson as was) had forgotten how cold it could be in March on the east coast of Scotland. "Raw" was the word her mother used when the east winds whistled around under heavy grey skies and the dampness went right through you. The hardest job on days like that had been keeping the coal fire stoked. Lizzie and her brothers and sisters always fought over the seat nearest the fire although it was only ever free when her father was out. Now the houses all had much-needed central heating. Lizzie was well wrapped up in her wheelchair but still she felt the chill. Her brothers James and Alex were at her side, her daughter Patty was pushing the chair and they were accompanied on their walk by her sister May's granddaughter Catherine, known as 'Cat', who had insisted on taking the day off school. Cat did not want to miss a minute of the excitement caused by her great-aunt's first visit to Scotland since leaving Fife at the age of 16, 69 years ago, to begin a new life in America. A spirited outgoing girl, she was always being told that she resembled Lizzie in nature. Her grandmother would hear of the almost constant arguments with her parents and shake her head, muttering 'just like Lizzie'. So Cat had been allowed to join them on their walk though the decision had caused yet another argument with her parents.

They were all walking along the High Street in the town where Lizzie and her brothers and sisters had been brought up. They had yet to reach the Anderson family home, but already Lizzie had recognised a lot. Her memories of her childhood were vivid and Patty never tired of hearing her mother recall stories of relatives and friends. Lizzie had not been in favour of Patty trying to contact the family she had long ago lost touch with. Even when Patty discovered her two brothers and two sisters were still alive Lizzie had not felt inclined to get in touch, far less visit them. Some things went too deep and perhaps they would not welcome her into their midst again. However now that she was here she had to admit she was glad Patty had insisted on booking the flights after the doctor had given her the green light to travel. Lizzie knew herself that her breathing could only worsen and that she would soon be dependent on oxygen as well as medication to get her through the days, so if there was ever a time to come home, this was it. The wheelchair had become a necessity in her life more than a year ago when her respiratory problems became so acute that she could no longer enjoy her weekly lunches with Patty, which were always followed by a visit to her favourite shopping mall to indulge in a much loved pastime, checking out the sale bargains. The one thing Lizzie had never lost was a love of clothes and nothing pleased her more than to buy a new outfit, with matching shoes of course. Her passion for shoes had never died, though nowadays the shoes had to be functional rather than fashionable.

When her brothers stopped outside No 249 which had been her home for the first 16 years of her life, Lizzie felt the tears come into her eyes. 'Is the house as you remember it Lizzie?', asked Alex. Lizzie could only look at them and nod. Patty put her hand on her mother's shoulder to comfort her. She knew how much this visit meant to her. When the stories of her mother's childhood had become more frequent and the tears came into her eyes more often, Patty decided to contact the local newspaper, the East Fife Reporter, to see if she could have a letter published asking for news of her aunts and uncles. The response had come quickly, though it had taken some time to persuade her mother to make the trip. Now though she was in no doubt it had been the right decision.

Lizzie remembered that money had never been plentiful at No 249 but there had always been food on the table and clothes on their backs and during the hard times in her life in America, and there had been lots of hard times, Lizzie had made sure her own children did not go without. She had drawn on her mother's experiences often. If only Lizzie and her father hadn't rowed so much but they had always been at loggerheads. When he had been invalided out of the Army and had to spend time convalescing at home the household had become a place of rows and tension. Peter Anderson had found it hard to come to terms with his enforced idleness and the small house with its five noisy children got on his nerves. Lizzie had never been a quiet, obedient child. Her mother described her as headstrong and obstinate and this caused many clashes. Being the oldest Lizzie bossed her brothers and sisters and was used to being the centre of attention until her father came home from the war and that all changed. Her younger sister May was his favourite. A very pretty girl with beautiful skin, rosy cheeks and long wavy hair, she was the opposite of the tall, bulky and wire haired Lizzie. The two girls competed for their father's attention but it was no contest, May always won hands down and was never happier than when she was sitting on her father's knee telling stories about Lizzie to get her into trouble.

Cat drawing her attention to the Co-operative Society store that they were now passing brought Lizzie's attention to the present. That was where the family had done most of their shopping, daily trips for 'the messages', and where most of their clothes and shoes had been bought. The store nowadays was a much reduced version of the one Lizzie remembered, but there was still a shoe department and Catherine was calling to her to come and see the shoes she wanted her mother to buy for her. Shoes had always been a favourite of Lizzie's and she asked Patty to push her to the window so that she could see them for herself. A pair of black mid-calf length thick soled boots, with lacing up the front seemed to be the culprit. Not very ladylike, but Lizzie had to admit the boots would probably fit right in with Cat's pierced ears, nose and tongue and her short spiky hairstyle. She could imagine that Cat's appearance would have caused confrontation between her and her parents. Perhaps they were more alike than Lizzie realised.

They walked on and Lizzie's memory slipped once again back to her childhood. As they came up to the church, Lizzie remembered the three girls, May, Mary and herself being dressed up for Sunday School and having two hours to fill before visiting relatives for Sunday tea. She had persuaded the other two to go with her to a local park to pick daisies and make daisychains, even though they had been warned to stay around the house and play and on no account to get dirty. May skipped alongside her, but as usual Mary trailed behind with a doleful expression, knowing this could only mean trouble but reluctant to be left out. No wonder they had nicknamed their youngest sister 'teary Mary'. She seemed to be constantly crying about something! By the time their father came to look for them the three girls were filthy. Daisychain making had become boring and they had ended up rolling down the hill in their best frocks. Being the eldest Lizzie got the blame of course and never did get any tea that day.

Life continued in that vein and when she became a teenager the rows with both her parents became more frequent and affected the whole family. Lizzie always wanted more. More fashionable clothes, particularly shoes. She wanted to wear make up, have her hair cut in the latest styles and her mother despaired of her wilful daughter.

Her father's brother, John Anderson, had emigrated to the USA as a young man and when he returned for a visit with his American wife Joan, Lizzie was ecstatic. She stuck like glue to her Aunt Joan's side. She never tired of listening to her American accent and her Aunt's clothes; well they were just what Lizzie wanted. By this time regular visits to the local Palace Cinema to watch the latest American movies had seduced Lizzie who spent most of her days dreaming of a life she did not know how she was going to get. The visit from her Aunt and Uncle only confirmed this. Aunt Joan had the latest permanent wave hairstyle, wore more make-up than anyone in Lizzie's immediate family did, and her shoes, well they were out of this world. Lizzie's favourite pair were snakeskin high heels and when her Aunt Joan allowed her to try them on, Lizzie was in seventh heaven. Never mind that she had to cram her feet into them and they pinched as she tottered along.

Her Uncle John had seen some of the scenes between her and her parents and had suggested that when Lizzie was 16 she should come to New Jersey to live with them for a couple of years and perhaps then she would be over this phase in her life and happy to return to Scotland. Lizzie knew nothing of this at the time, but shortly after her 16th birthday there had been another almighty row between her and her parents when Lizzie had locked her sister Mary in the coal cellar for no other reason than that she had been 'getting on her nerves'. The fact that Mary had been crying so much she had been incoherent when Lizzie finally relented and let her out and had to be put straight to bed didn't help Lizzie's cause. Her father announced that she was being 'sent' to New Jersey to stay with her Uncle John and Aunt Joan. They would find her a job and she would send money home to help her family in Fife. Lizzie was unsure about being 'sent' to America and what was in store for her there. This was not what she envisaged; sending her hard earned money back to Scotland was not in her plans, but she went along with everything. If this was how she could get to a new life in the USA, then so be it.

Arrangements were made and Lizzie was due to sail from Glasgow to New York in the summer of 1930, aged 16. She was so excited. Her mother was already packing a trunk with gifts to take to her Aunt and Uncle, as well as some new clothes for Lizzie herself. Lizzie was determined to choose her leaving outfit herself and eventually wore her parents down and had been allowed to visit the Ladies Department in the Co-operative Society on her own. She had chosen a dove grey summer dress and when she went into the shoe department to match up a pair of shoes, what did they have there but a pair of snakeskin high heels. Well maybe they were not real snakeskin and they certainly did not match the dress, but to Lizzie they were just what she wanted and she was determined to have them. Was that not what every woman in America wore after all and she wanted to fit right in.

She knew what her parents' reaction would be and they did not disappoint her. Her father was furious about the shoes, but the store was closed and they were leaving the next morning so there was nothing he could do about it. Lizzie went off to bed the happiest of people that night. When she woke next morning to get dressed she was horrified to discover that her longed for pair of 'high heeled' shoes were now 'flats'. Her father's final act had been to cut off the heels while she slept. She was devastated. Did he hate her so much?

The rest was history. Lizzie knew as she boarded the bus for Glasgow with her mother that whatever happened she would not return to Fife. When her Uncle John met her in New York she asked him to take her to the nearest shoe shop where she bought another pair of high heels. This was soon followed by a permanent wave and make-up and Lizzie's life in America began. It had not been the easiest of lives and she had initially kept in touch with her family, but after her second marriage broke up and she moved to California with her children in tow she knew her mother would never have approved of her lifestyle and she just stopped writing.

Lizzie was looking forward to a family tea at May's home and with a smile she urged Patty, Cat, James and Alex to get a move on, she needed a heat and a cup of tea. Enough reminiscences for one day! Lizzie had been amazed to discover that her sister May had been the one who had tried hardest to discover her whereabouts in California. May, who had been her childhood rival, had welcomed her and Patty into her home.

Now she knew it had been a mistake to let something so simple as a pair of shoes cloud her memories of her family. Thank God Patty had brought her home at last. She still had time to get to know her brothers and sisters all over again, and she must remember to have a word with that great-niece of hers, Cat, to make sure she didn't follow too closely in her great-aunt's footsteps.

A Life in the Day of a Crematorium Organ

By William Clinkenbeard

You won't believe what I'm going to tell you. I know you won't, but I will anyway. I am so fed up that I have to talk to somebody. The boss has a break now, so I'm not working. The assembly line has stopped. There is no service for the next half-hour. In-on-down, in-on-down—that's the way it goes on all day here.

I am a first-class pipe organ. Not an electronic and not a computer organ, but a genuine pipe organ. I am a beautiful instrument, capable of being played anywhere—in the Usher Hall or any good concert hall. But here I am, pushed into the corner of this gloomy chapel in a crematorium. There are no windows here, only a tapestry picturing trees and plants and animals. It's always dark in here, and the chapel has an aroma that will adhere to my pipes forever. The smell is always there, even after the attendant goes around spraying his little aerosol can of air freshener. You may have come here once or twice, probably even oftener if you are getting on a bit. But you have no idea what it feels like to be stuck here day after day doing a dead-end job. From nine to five every day I play funereal music that kills the spirit.

I didn't know it would be like this when I took this job. OK, you may say that I should have known what I was getting into when I went to work in a crematorium. But I assumed naturally that people would want good music, music that speaks profoundly to the experience of death. Is that so illogical? Boy, was I wrong! OK, I'm not the most modest of organs, I admit. I suppose that I have a high opinion of myself. But several organists have backed me up on this; they have played me and said that I was very good.

What I mean is that I am capable of so much more. I can play Bach, Beethoven or Brahms. I can do Handel, Mendelssohn or Buxtehude. I can even play Vidor on a good day. I have an action and a sound that is second to none. All this beautiful music I can do. But no, I get other things to play, music you would not believe....Hold on, there is a service coming in, the line is moving again, and the boss is on the bench. I'll need to get to work, if that is what you call it.

Oh No, not again! It's the Co-op Double Bill—*The Lord's My Shepherd* and *Abide with Me*. You know that if the hymnbooks in this place are dropped they fall open automatically to these two. Some days I feel that if I have to play them yet again, I will scream. Well, burst a stop really. If the people ever thought seriously about the words to hymns—like *He makes me down to lie*—as far as the deceased is concerned he certainly was made down to lie. But I doubt that he ever saw a sheep or a shepherd, only the top flat up some close somewhere. And as far as *Abide with Me* is concerned, I personally would be happy to *point you to the skies and push you off.* Honestly, can people not choose some really good hymns, ones that haven't been ruined by overkill? I mean, there must be about five hundred hymns in the book that no one ever sings!

I confess to you though that sometimes I get a laugh, but only quietly to myself to preserve my sanity. The pub crowd comes in surrounded by a cloud of smoke, dressed mostly in black leather jackets, and they are aching to sing *The Old Rugged Cross.* I know that they like it, but the truth is that they sing it far better after a few pints than they do in here. They may well sing about a *world of lost sinners*, but they wouldn't ever consider themselves sinners. The Boss is always kidding about how they sing *let us with a glass of wine* instead of *let us with a gladsome mind.* That's his little and only joke.

Sometimes I also get a laugh from the bowling club crowd when they come in to say goodbye to one of their members. They are better behaved than the pub crowd but they always want to sing *Once in Royal David's City* even when it isn't Christmas. And it's just because of the last line—*when like stars his children crowned, all in white shall wait around.* They say it takes them straight to the bowling green.

I know that you won't believe me, but I just have to tell you this. We once had a service for a guy who had died in prison. He was quite popular, and so the chapel was filled with prisoners. There were all kinds of prison officers and guards here as well. Boy, were they nervous. Some of the lifers were handcuffed to the guards. Well, do you know what they sang? *Lord, dismiss us with your blessing!* I knew you wouldn't believe it.

And when the ex-Boy's Brigade members come in, they want to sing *Will your anchor hold?* That's entirely natural of course, and it's not a bad hymn. But it slays me when they come to the line *Steadfast and sure while the billows roll.* I mean, do you know what a *billow* is? Does anybody? I can just see the headline in the newspaper some day: *A local man, while walking on the foreshore at Granton, was suddenly washed away by a billow.* Everyone would say to themselves: What? What is a billow?

I guess it's lunchtime. The boss has his sandwiches out on my keyboard again. I really hate this. There are breadcrumbs and flakes of cheese wedged down between my keys. Surely he could at least use good brown bread for his sandwiches. I've got a circle stain on my top where he puts his flask of coffee. Worse still, he is resting this paperback on me yet again. I can't abide Dick Francis. You should hear the organ tuner curse under his breath when he comes to tune me. He is about the only one who understands how I feel.

Mind you, I feel sorry for the boss as well. He gets bored out of his mind. He is a good musician; I can tell by the way he strokes me. He has nice hands and a sensitive touch. His pedal work is OK as well. But he is stuck here just like me. Did you know that he has a Master Degree in Music? He did his thesis on Bach's work for the organ. Now all he does is play for funerals. All those beautiful toccatas and fugues just reside in his brief case going yellow with age. Of course, he does have his Sunday work in the church. At least he has a little more scope there, but I sit here totally on my own and unplayed on a Sunday. So it isn't much better than Monday through Saturday.

Speaking of church, I can tell you that some of the ministers who come here to take funerals are pathetic. The fundamentalist type, I mean. They rant and rave and go on about the cross and the blood of the lamb. They always use crucifixion hymns for the service. I guess they don't believe in the resurrection. They go on past the half-hour limit all the time, and so the whole assembly line operation gets held up. They don't seem to have a sense of humour or any real humanity. I certainly wouldn't want to go to their version of heaven, assuming of course that there is a heaven for organs. You would still be singing about the cross up there.

On the other hand, some of the best services take place when lots of church folk are here. They know the hymns and can sing them. When that happens I really feel lifted up and can do my best. You may talk about the organ supporting the singing, but it works the other way round too. I need to be supported by the people.

Well, here we go. Time to get back to work. The line is moving again—in-on-down. Oh, hold on. I see I'm not required for this service. I can take a break. The music is all on tape. It's the latest addition to the place—the tape machine. I suppose that being honest, my nose isn't really out of joint. If they don't want good music then they might as well have the canned variety. At least it's better than *The Old Rugged Cross*. But you would be amazed at what some people ask for. I remember one lady whose husband had died very suddenly. She asked for some Spanish flamenco-type piece. I suppose they had heard it on holiday. But the Boss had never heard of it, having never been to Spain. With his salary he can just about manage Portobello. Anyway, when he said he didn't know that piece, she asked for *Are You Lonesome Tonight?* To give the Boss credit, he just said 'No.' Well that isn't quite true. In fact, he said that he didn't have the music. So she brought in a tape to play. Can you imagine hearing *Are You Lonesome Tonight?* during your husband's funeral service? I felt like saying: 'No, he's OK. He's got Elvis to keep him company.'

Then we had someone who wanted us to play a tape for the postlude after his wife's service. He brought in *I want to go out in a blaze of glory*. Well, I guess that she did, at least in a blaze. It is a crematorium after all. That's what the boys down below are there for. But there was one even worse than that. Somebody once brought in a tape of piano plus vocal music. I mean, it was nicely done—Nat King Cole as I remember. But what do you think about *Pick yourself up, dust yourself off, and start all over again*? Unbelievable right? I mean, it is pretty optimistic isn't it? If it were my own service, I would ask for *I gotta get outta this place if it's the last thing I ever do*. However, I suppose that in a few years I will be redundant anyway. It will all be taped music. So instead of the Co-op Double Bill it will be the Crem Top Twenty.

Well, thank God, that is about it for the day. I couldn't take much more. Just one more service and the line can stop rolling. I'll be glad to call it a day even if I haven't played anything interesting. The folk are all seated in the chapel, and the coffin is ready to be brought in. Wait a minute! Hang on! What is this he's playing on me? It can't be! Widor's Toccata? Yes, it is, and it's a good tempo. I can't believe it. He's got all my stops out, full volume. This is magnificent. But I'll have to stop soon because the coffin is in place, the flowers have been laid and the minister is ready to speak. But we aren't stopping! The Boss has flipped. He's gone over the top. I knew that he was in a worse state than me. He is playing on and on. This is wonderful! 'Go for it, Boss', I hear myself saying. He's flipped, but I don't mind. For once we're doing it properly. We're going to put some life into death.

A Circle Closed

By Anne Ewing

I stood by the window, looking out on to a mundane and unaccountably forlorn sight, a small, colourless, awkwardly shaped yard, occupied only by a few cars, parked more or less within badly faded white lines. On that bright June day, the late afternoon sun had already dipped behind the dismal 1960's vintage concrete and glass extension that housed the room I was in, leaving the yard in surprisingly deep shade. The angle made by this newer part of the building and its much older, more substantial, stone-built counterpart enclosed a stoory corner where a miniature dust-devil was birling some old leaves in papery, whispering circles. Directly opposite, a few shallow steps led up to a doorway whose lintel bore, in bas-relief, the word: INFANTS. Its leaf strewn and cobwebby appearance suggested that it was a long time since it had been used. The remainder of the yard was enclosed by a stone wall, which on one side merged into the gently sloping slate roof of the old school house, and on the adjacent side was surmounted by vertical black iron railings.

Beyond the closed door of the room I occupied, could be heard a variety of sounds, some of human origin, but most electronic in nature. The most penetrating of these were the 'zit-zoot' of a frantic printer, the cheerful 'ta-da' of a computer greeting and the irritating, persistent ring of an unanswered telephone. More intermittently discernible were the occasional sounds of footsteps in the corridor, sometimes with accompanying voices in passing conversation, a spasmodic, barking cough from the office next door and, underlying it all, the more or less continuous, soporific drone of a lecturing voice from the classroom on the other side.

I was alone in a room with which I was very familiar, but from which I felt increasingly alienated. I had come to hate the hastily-erected shelving, haphazardly filled with books and files, the blank-fronted filing cabinets, filled, I knew, with bulging folders, badly arranged and forever inaccessible, even if anyone wanted to consult them, which I found more and more unlikely. On the floor lay a number of ankle-bruising plastic storage boxes, full of the detritus of courses and lessons, perhaps in readiness, but more likely at this stage of the term, already delivered and dumped here, awaiting emptying and filing.

The contents of the room gave rise to a nose-wrinkling smell of dust and a vague sense of decay. In a word, it was foosty. As a child, I had spent most of my Saturday sixpence on some item of stationery. I always loved notebooks, pens, pencils, crayons and rubbers. As a newly-qualified teacher, I would relish each visit to the stationery cupboard, where I would inhale a furtive fix of that heady, but astringent mixture of paper, wood, paint, wax and ink that emanated from the neat piles of jotters, stacked boxes of writing and drawing materials and packets of pristine white paper, some for writing and copying, others of the heavy cartridge variety for drawing and painting. The most alluring of all were the towers of multicoloured card in sequential rainbow patterns, soaring, it seemed, to the ceiling. My present surroundings, in their sorry, dilapidated state, were the very antithesis of this long-remembered vision of ordered perfection.

As a place of work, the room was less than inspiring and always dispiriting, and I was invariably grateful that it only technically fulfilled that purpose for me, weekly attendance at a department meeting my sole obligation to be there. Otherwise, I worked in schools, supporting children, individually or in small groups, their teachers and parents. The peripatetic (or 'pretty pathetic' as I sometimes self-deprecatingly thought of it!) nature of my job was difficult in the early days, as I felt somewhat rootless and homeless. But, as time passed and I came to be accepted and welcome in most of my schools, I began to feel relieved not to be involved in the inevitable power struggles or personality clashes unavoidable in any one establishment.

There was no doubt that I felt at home in a school environment and always had, a necessary pre-requisite, one might assume, for the choice of teaching as a career. But I had come to know only too well, that the cynicism and antipathy felt by many teachers, came to outweigh, with the passage of years, the happy anticipation and vocational impulse that had initially impelled them to embark on a career in education. It seemed to me that the dashing of hopes and its accompanying destruction of morale was paralleled by the physical transformation that had been visited upon this very building. I had come to realise that the reason I disliked it so much was that it was no longer a school. I was uncertain of my function within its walls. What was expected of me here?

That had not always been the case, but it seemed as if that was another life, in another dimension entirely.

When it ceased to be a school, it was reincarnated as a staff development and resources centre. Teachers, logic dictated, came there to be 'developed'. To that end, I would sometimes help to run in-service courses where my department's expertise was supposedly disseminated to other mainstream teachers, who, having thus been 'developed' would, in turn, 'cascade' this 'enhancement' to others in their schools. There was always a great deal of 'overarching' and 'underpinning' involved in creating a 'raft of good practice'. This terminology, or to be more truthful, jargon, or even gobbledegook, invoking, for some reason, metaphors of watery construction, poured forth from the top of the hierarchical pyramid that education seemed to have become, namely, St Andrew's House as was, or the Scottish Executive as it now is. It trickled, sparkling and crystal clear all the way down to the labouring masses at the chalkface. I always suspected that the clarity of the comprehension achieved in all this 'development' was more closely related to mud than to crystal, but the effect of it all was to fill forests of paper with documents, initiatives, policies, plans and programmes. It also clogged up the ether with immeasurable torrents of electrically generated and communicated information, but the promised 'paperless office' remained as far away as ever, as witnessed by those bloated and costive filing cabinets in evidence in every part of that building.

So much for development! What about resources? In my case, they comprised two types: The first represented by the language teaching books, of theory and practice, the communication strategies and games, the rolled-up pictures and posters now filling, in no perceived order, those rickety shelves. Much, if not all of it, was dated, dreary, dog-eared and dingy. The second consisted of the reams of worksheets I and my colleagues had laboured over to produce ourselves, at no cost to the education authority. These we shared, or not, in the case of those teachers who kept their creative efforts close, even copy-righted, to their chests. These were costly for us in terms of the time and effort involved and, on reflection, I realise, compared well with the commercially produced materials which were available but which were too expensive, in times of budgetary restraint as decreed by national government, and the consequent belt-tightening required of education authorities. So many teachers were forced, not only to produce much of their resources, but to buy their own books and materials.

Involvement in bureaucratic procedures had become an integral part of any teaching job description. For every hour spent imparting information, or interacting with the pupils in all aspects of their learning, which, after all, represents the real essence of teaching, at least one hour had to be spent in writing plans for what that would entail, and in evaluating and reporting on its outcomes. All the paper thus generated would of course join the rest in one of those overfed cabinets I have already described, there to reside for all time or until someone, perhaps H.M.I., asked to see it, which ever came first!

As I stood alone in that dusty and depressing room, with these even more depressing thoughts in mind, I tried to summon up the sense of relief and imminent liberation that I knew I should have. The fact was, that within a few days I would be free forever of all these burdens involved in developing and resourcing myself and my job. I would be able to listen to news of the latest planned educational initiative with equanimity. As a retired teacher I would be free to pass disinterested but polite comment only if I chose to do so. But I could not throw off a feeling of regret that I would no longer have a stake in education in general or teaching in particular. My own sons were adults, the years of school, university and post-graduate study long behind them, and with no grandchildren in prospect, why should I care or worry? Turning from contemplation of the source of my depression to the window again, I had my answer.

The cars in the playground had gone, but it was no longer empty and featureless, the door no longer a rarely used emergency exit tightly closed against the world. Instead, it was open and welcoming to two crocodiles of small children one of boys and one of girls, waiting expectantly to enter the school. Another group of even younger children stood to one side, most holding tightly to the hands of their mothers. Some of these young women were as smartly turned out as lingering post-war austerity would allow, the vestiges of a watered-down New Look in evidence in the long, widely flaring hemlines of their coats. Others were dressed in hastily donned coats of a more workaday style, thrown over the ubiquitous floral wrap-around peenies favoured by housewives of that era. In a few cases, big brothers and sisters had been entrusted with conducting their younger siblings to school for the first time.

As a hand rung bell sounded in the adjoining playground, summoning the older children from a morass of running, shouting and squealing bodies into an ordered pattern of lines, a teacher suddenly appeared in the infants' doorway. At the sight of this newcomer on the scene, an expectant hush fell on the assembled group of little ones. One little girl with a jaunty yellow ribbon in her fair hair, which belied her shy and anxious demeanour as she stood close to her mother, now did her best to disappear completely, squirming closely into the back of her mother's coat.

It came to me as I watched that scene in the playground, that I was that little girl and that this was my first day at school, the first day of the new school session in August 1951. At a word from the teacher at the top of the steps, the two lines of waiting children, now proud and confident primary two veterans, marched into the school, as the nervous new recruits and their almost as anxious guardians were ushered by the small but formidable figure of Miss Paterson into the drill hall, where Miss Oliphant, or Miss Elephant, as some of her new little charges would mistakenly but innocently address her, was waiting to enrol them into her new Primary One class. As this procedure was accomplished, each newly registered pupil was shown to their classroom, where they were quickly left by their mothers, sisters or brothers. Long goodbyes were firmly discouraged by the indomitable aforementioned Miss Paterson who had left her own Primary Three class to be combined with another for the morning as she helped to settle the new entrants, while Miss Oliphant completed the enrolment process.

As was customary in those days, primary schools were staffed almost exclusively by maiden ladies. The only male figures in school were usually those at either end of the hierarchy, namely the janitor and the headmaster, neither of which posts could reasonably be entrusted to a woman! Female teachers were expected to give up their jobs if and when they married, when they accepted the financial security of matrimony in lieu of that of paid employment, there being no apparent need for both. It was not until later in the 1950's that this policy began to change. Miss Paterson was typical of that breed of spinster infant teacher, the mainstay of elementary teaching in those days.

She was tiny, but carried herself so well that every inch counted. Her countenance was one of severity and exactitude. There was never a hair of her neatly coiffured head out of place. She wore no make-up but had a well-scrubbed complexion, and always smelled subtly but unmistakably of lily-of-the-valley. She invariably wore a neat tweed skirt, with a blouse in summer and a fine wool jumper or twin-set in winter. These were rarely glimpsed garments, as they were usually covered by a button-through, three-quarter length overall of some discreet and tasteful floral print. It had long, wide sleeves ending in tightly buttoned cuffs and the collar was fastened by a brooch—sometimes a cream and coral cameo or a Scottish semi-precious stone in a Celtic silver setting. No-nonsense lisle-thread brown stockings and well polished sensible brown lacing shoes completed her image of solidity and dependability. No-one ever argued with Miss Paterson. Many of those mothers who left their wee ones in her charge had been pupils of hers one generation earlier, and while they may have been struggling with lumps in their throats or incipient tears in their eyes, as they resisted the impulse to linger or to cast a backward glance as they made their way out of the classroom, they had the consolation of knowing that their bairns were in the safest of hands.

I was one of those bairns, the wee girl with the yellow ribbon, and my memory of that day and the happy and not so happy ones, of the early months of schooling in the same building as I was standing in fifty years later, serves me well. But for some reason, I do not remember seeing my mother leave. I was too engrossed in studying my new surroundings. The high ceilinged room had sickly, green panelling extending more than half way up the walls, the remainder of which were painted a dingy cream. Most of this, however, was obliterated by a myriad of pictures and posters, cards and charts. There were Biblical scenes, similar to the ones found on too few pages of our Bible at home, a world map, much of which was stained British Empire pink. A series of cards displayed the numbers one to ten. Each had the numeral, the word and the corresponding colour-coded dots to represent the number. The letters of the alphabet, days of the week, months and seasons of the year, pictures and names of animals and everyday objects and weather words and pictures festooned the friezes which ran around the top of the wood panelling. So many images, colours and ideas, bewildering in their novelty and variety gave me, in a few brief minutes, the promise of a whole new dimension to my young life. This prospect of an entire, new undreamed of world engulfed me to the exclusion of all else, until my attention was suddenly wrenched back to my immediate situation.

I sensed my fleeting exhilaration drain down into the very toes of my new school shoes, as I reverted to being that scared wee lassie who had so recently clung to the shelter of her mother's skirts in the playground, and I took stock of my new companions. The little infant-scaled desks and chairs were lined up in uncompromisingly regular lines and the one I sat at, like all the others, faced the overwhelming presence of *the teacher*. I realised then that it was her surprisingly loud and insistent voice that had called me back from the threshold of that enticing, new world I had tantalisingly glimpsed. Her attention was directed, not at me, but at the wee boy sitting immediately to my right. His eyes were brimming with tears, and his lower lip trembled alarmingly as he strove manfully not to break down completely. He had clearly been told that 'big boys don't cry' and was doing his best to comply with that directive. I don't know if perhaps I gave the appearance of being about to come out in sympathy with wee James Thomson, but I was suddenly aware that Miss Paterson's implacable stare had swivelled towards me with the very strong suggestion that 'You're not going to cry, are you, Helen?' Much as I felt like it, I didn't dare give vent to the feeling of abandonment that had overwhelmed me in those few moments. Something told me that my fate was sealed, and there was nothing I could do about it. This was school and I had better get used to it. But more than that, I seemed to sense that I was in my element. The excitement and attraction that beckoned from all sides on the walls of the classroom, far outweighed the trepidation inspired in me by the all-pervading presence of the teacher or the shyness and anxiety I felt in relation to my peers.

In those days, there were no mother and toddler groups or playgoups, and little or no nursery school provision, no sensitive, gradual induction into the world of education, no pre-enrolment visit to prepare you for that first day in class. My situation was exacerbated by the fact that I lived with my family on a farm, three miles from the village primary school. In terms of the contrast in lifestyle with my townie peers, it might as well have been three hundred! Apart from my big sister and some cousins we played with very occasionally, I had had no contact with other children until I found myself incarcerated that day with many other boys and girls of whom, apart from wee James Thomson, I was only now becoming fully aware.

Having succeeded in forestalling an epidemic of tears, Miss Paterson soon had us engaged in various activities which had the desired effect of distracting us from the absence of our mothers and our presence in this alien if fascinating environment. I remember a sand tray where I could trace pictures with my fingers, and coloured beads, which had to be threaded onto strings following the colour sequence displayed on a card. Building bricks, jigsaws, sorting trays of little coloured items comprised some of the paraphernalia of pre-reading and pre-number learning tasks masquerading as toys and games which occupied us for the first few days of school. But it was not long until this all gave way to the serious business of mastering the first steps along the road to literacy and numeracy, when sums calculated with chalk on little slates and blackboards in time gave way to the squared pages of arithmetic jotters and the little cards with single words kept in an old tobacco tin to the first real and much coveted reading book.

None of this held any terrors for me, as I took to the business of learning with enthusiasm and delight. Of course, much had rubbed off on me from my big sister Jean, and her four years experience of school. What was much harder for me was the entire matter of the social adjustment necessary to get to grips with the human elements of my new environment. As is often the case, it was much more difficult to learn to negotiate the obstacles and minefields of the playground and the school bus, than it was to survive the well-ordered and supervised classroom. Jean often came to my rescue, as she firmly dealt with attempts by anyone to bully me, until I eventually learned, fitfully and painfully, to stand up for myself amongst my classmates and the older pupils, some of whom had an unerring instinct for targeting the shyer and overly sensitive youngsters among the new school intake.

Time in the playground in the mornings, at playtime and dinner-time was filled with what seemed initially like an impenetrable mayhem of running, shouting, pushing and shoving, none of which made any sense to me. By and large, it seemed that girls and boys played separately, but some games were common to both groups. Tig was a year-round favourite and easy to understand in principle, but its more sophisticated versions were beyond our comprehension and for wee ones, even the simplest running to catch or to avoid being caught often ended in skinned knees and bumped heads. Other games would appear in their turn, when they would occupy almost the entire school population for a spell. Some were seasonally or climatically determined. Autumn was conker time, but this seemed exclusively reserved for the bigger boys, and as such was imbued with a mystique, which would forever elude my understanding. Similarly, some of the older girls had wondrous collections of various kinds. Some were fairly obvious and easy to aspire to, like paper scraps, some purchased, some cut out of magazines and papers, but others, more esoteric in their nature fascinated me. Piggy collections, which consisted of small pieces of broken pottery or china would be pored over and pieces swapped and bartered almost as a currency. Where did they find these treasures in such quantity?

Winter playground fun terrified and excited me in equal measure. Snow brought the terrors of snowball fights, which were the province of older bairns, but wee ones would often be the unintended targets of badly aimed snowballs. Even worse was the horror of having your face deliberately rubbed with handfuls of snow, or worst of all sharp, scratchy ice. Hard-packed snow or even rime and frost on the playground provided ideal conditions for making ice slides. The older boys and girls would start the process in the mornings, hone the slides to lethal shine and speed at playtime and enjoy a full dinner hour of slippery, frenzied fun, which we infants could only stand and watch longingly from the sidelines. But our chance came at home time, which preceded that of the older classes, when we could have a few minutes of thrillingly illicit sliding, provided, of course that a treacherous rise in temperature or an even more deadly Jannie with a bucketful of sand and salt hadn't put paid to the slide in the meantime!

As a primary one infant with a sister four years and, it seemed, a lifetime ahead of me, I was very impatient to acquire all her social skills and practical abilities. She wasn't afraid of anyone—boy or girl—of any size, and she could do all the things, apparently effortlessly, that I longed to be able to master, and struggled hard to manage. One such new skill was that of skipping. Initially it was a solitary activity, using a short rope, bought for the purpose, with a handle at either end. But what really attracted me, and I longed to be old—and big—enough to join in, were the skipping games with the older girls. They required a much longer rope that would have to be begged, borrowed or even on occasion, stolen from home, as was the fate of many a mother's washing line. In these games, two girls would ca' or turn either end of this long rope. The longer the rope, the more girls could be 'in' at the same time, and sometimes as many as seven or eight could be jumping at the same time. They would jump in and skip along the rope, leave and go round the back of the ca'ers to re-enter and jump the other way. It all required a great deal of skill and a good sense of rhythm and timing, which could only be achieved by lots of practice.

I despaired of ever having the chance to learn, as the older girls would look down on us wee ones with disdain. We were a pain in the neck, as we hadn't mastered the skill of jumping in the turning rope. If the owner of the rope, and, consequently the controller of the game, could be persuaded to allow you a turn, they would do a 'wavy' for you. You would have to stand close beside the stationary rope and the ca'ers would move it slowly backwards and forwards a few times, so that you could time your first jump correctly as they moved the rope all the way round. With a bit of luck and practice, you might then be able to keep going as they kept the rope turning, but more often I remember such requests being turned down. 'Awa' ye go. There's nae wavies the day!' I was always delighted when Jean managed to acquire a rope from the farm, and she would sometimes accede to my desperate pleas to be included, even if only for a few minutes, in the big girls' skipping games. I loved the rhymes, songs and chants that accompanied the skipping, to the rhythm of the beating rope.

'On yonder hill, there stands a lady,
Who she is I do not know.

All she wants is gold and silver,
All she wants is a nice young man.
Call in my sister Jean, sister Jean, sister Jean,
Call in my sister Jean, and I'll skip out and leave her'.
So a new jumper would join the rope as the last one left at the other end.

As the boys played football, so the girls had their own, more sedate but no less skilful ball games. Starting with one rubber ball and gradually progressing to two, we would play simple games of throw and catch, but as our dexterity improved, we would play increasingly complicated games of throwing, and bouncing the ball against a wall, simultaneously performing a variety of actions before catching it again. These ball games were also accompanied by singing or chanting rhymes like:

'Charlie Chaplin went to France,
To teach the ladies how to dance.
First the heel and then the toe,
And then you do big birlie o!'

This last movement required you to turn yourself around in a complete circle while the ball was in the air, catching it before it hit the ground. The successful completion of this manoeuvre was without doubt the absolute pinnacle of accomplishment.

Experience has taught me that each stage in life brings its share of trauma and anxiety, but I will never forget the sheer agony I suffered on occasion in the course of that first year of school. Some was of a chronic variety that stemmed basically, I now realise, although I couldn't have seen the connection then, from the fact that I lived on a farm, which imposed inevitable practical limitations on my lifestyle. The first of these to impinge on my consciousness was when the time came for my first school Christmas party. As country mice, we couldn't go home for dinner, so had to arrive dressed in our glad rags, such as they were, first thing in the morning, whereas the town, and therefore infinitely more glamorous and alluring mice, lived near enough the school to get changed at lunch time. This was the first time I experienced the 'oohing' and 'aahing' that went on in the playground as each one returned to school. When urged with sufficient persuasion, she would coyly open her coat to reveal her party wear. This would sometimes amount to a froth of tulle, or net, as we called it or even some sequined or similarly sparkly confection.

Most achingly envied of all, though, were the contents of the casually held brown paper parcels which some of the girls carried. I just knew that they contained silver or gold party shoes, the like of which I could only dream about possessing, and sure enough they could be seen later fussily changing into this fabulous footwear in the cloakroom, as we mere mortals looked on. Somehow I knew that, even if I had the fanciest, most glittery, party dress in the world, I would never enjoy the opportunity to make an entrance like that. Arriving dressed for the party first thing in the morning in some subtle way lacked the impact that was guaranteed by the anticipation of the celebration to come that had built up by the middle of the day. Added to this was the perennial handicap we laboured under, that our mother never bought us frivolous party frocks, favouring instead, well tailored serviceable home-made garments that could see service for a variety of social occasions, and not just an annual shindig. In contrast, there seemed to be very few times when our status as farm children gave us any kind of edge over our classmates. The kudos to be gained from being asked, every year by the teacher, come harvest time, to bring into school some stalks of oats, barley and wheat, so that we could learn about the differences in the three grains, paled into insignificance when compared with the chance to shine in the glamour stakes!

If I sensed, even at that early age, a degree of social disadvantage that resulted from living in the country, it was as nothing compared with the almost insurmountable problem of developing a social life acceptable to both me and my parents, as a teenager. Now, of course, with the benefit of hindsight, I realise how fortunate it was that I had a farm upbringing—lucky for me in that I had more healthy freedom, fresh air and fun than I might have had growing up in the town, and even luckier for my parents, because when I was home from school, I was home, and automatically protected from many of the dangers and temptations I might have been exposed to in an urban setting. At the time, of course, I did not see it that way, and I would have done almost anything to live in the town and be like everyone else, a natural adolescent desire not to be seen as different in any way, but to merge into the background with everyone else. Given my hyper-sensitivity to my rural origins, I have always hated with a vengeance the saying, and the sentiments it expressed, 'You can take the girl out of the country, but you can't take the country out of the girl'.

A more acute and consequently more powerful, though thankfully, short-lived agony came that same afternoon of the first school party. We had been instructed to bring a cup and saucer from home for our cup of tea that would accompany the cakes and sandwiches we were provided with at the party. How vastly different from the catering arrangements that would be made for little ones nowadays! I must have been conscious of the need for keeping up appearances, as I insisted on having one from my mother's limited supply of fine crockery. While gracious living did not come high on the agenda of farm life, the one she gave me definitely came into the category of 'guid cheenie', and I was warned to look after it, as it was wrapped carefully, first in newspaper and then in brown paper and string. Of course, my being clumsy and the 'cheenie' being fragile, the inevitable happened, and I dropped and broke the cup before it could even be filled with tea. I was inconsolable, not because the party was from that moment ruined for me, but because I believed my mother would be forever bereft for want of her pretty cup. No amount of reassurance from Miss Oliphant would persuade me that it was not, in fact, the end of the world. I sensed that my mother did not have many lovely things, and regretted deeply being the cause of her losing one of them, all because of my concern with social etiquette. If I couldn't have a party dress, I was determined to have a nice cup for my tea! Of course, I realised later that the most precious things for my mother, the least pretentious person I would ever know, were not things at all, but people, particularly me, my sister and our father.

If there were agonies, there was ecstasy too, associated with the playground that first Christmas at school. I had made rapid progress in reading and began to be able to recognise letters and their sounds, and to realise that I could attempt to decipher words and their significance beyond the scope of my reading book. One morning at playtime, as I stood in the playground by the railings, I saw a lorry pass the school with the letters N.C.B. painted on the side. Of more immediate interest to me was the sight of its cargo—a pile of Christmas trees! As tenants on a farm owned by the National Coal Board, I was used to seeing lorries like this come to the farm from time to time. I knew that one of the perks we enjoyed, and no doubt the one that least excited or enriched my parents, was that each year we were given a Christmas tree. The remainder of that day was spent in a fever of unspoken excitement. Was one of those trees destined for us? I hugged this glorious expectation to myself, savouring the renewed thrill it gave me each time my mind returned to speculate on the possibility. My excitement grew as we travelled home in the school bus, which had never gone so slowly, but still not a word about Christmas trees passed my lips. I dared not ask Dad as he picked us up in the landrover at the end of the farm road, but waited in an agony of anticipation until I tumbled out of the vehicle and hurried across the close. As I ran round the corner of the porch, there it was! Propped up against the back door was the most beautiful Christmas tree I have ever seen. The sense of a moment of utter perfection and contentment that comes from a hope fulfilled returns to me every time I see an unadorned Christmas tree and smell its bare piney foliage, still redolent in its cold greenness, of its home in the forest, as it waits to be transformed into a symbol of annually renewed joy that never fails to lift the heart and enrich the soul. The words, 'It's the most beautiful tree we have ever had' spoken every year invariably remind me of that tree long ago that rewarded a wee girl's trust so richly.

The vividly clear pictures that had filled my mind as I stood in that dreary room began to fade as I realised that the gloom in the deserted playground was deeper than ever. The cars recently parked there had gone, their drivers unseen by me as, lost in memories, I had retraced the early months of my life in and around this building that had been my first school. Though much changed in appearance and function, it was still the place where I took my first faltering steps on a road that had eventually, after many twists and turns, brought me back to my starting point. Although my working life was nearly over, the spirit of that wee girl had remained unchanged. We were separated only by time, a summer holiday short of fifty years. I had my answer. No matter how much the context of teaching and learning had changed over that span of time, the essence would remain the same. There would always be children who loved learning, and teachers who loved teaching. The little girl I had been would always play in that playground, and I knew I would for ever retain the joy and delight I felt now, as I saw her for the last time. She ran up the steps to the first of the many doorways she would encounter on her journey, turned, and with a shy smile, waved briefly before disappearing inside.

Bees, Mushrooms and Hedgehogs

By Allan Moore

I brought my new Rudge bicycle up on the train from Manchester. I had to leave it in the guard's van. Finding a seat in the compartment next to the van and on the corridor side allayed my anxiety. I could now relax until the train reached Carlisle, where I had to change trains and board the train for Aspaitria to meet the people I would be staying with for some weeks.

After the short journey to Aspaitria, I struggled with my bike and case along to the ticket barrier. A woman accompanied by a girl of about twelve years old came forward and introduced herself as my new Aunt Esme' and my cousin June. The clothes they wore were good quality but dated.

'Follow us,' she commanded. They set off up over a metal bridge which spanned two lines, to a waiting train. Keeping up with my aunt and cousin was quite difficult, the case was heavy and my cycle seemed to have a mind of its' own. I secured the bike in the guard's van and then joined them some way down the train. The train was non-corridor, so I lowered the window at each of the many stops, to check that no one made off with my bike. Aunt Esme' looked irritated at my concern but did concede that it looked expensive.

The nearest station to our destination was Gilcrux. On arrival, Aunt Esme' insisted that I handed my return ticket over to her for safekeeping and my case was left to be delivered later that day. Aunt Esme' and June retrieved their bikes which were propped up against a wall along with many others, an amazing collection of old boneshakers and flying bedsteads. Having a shining new bike was like wearing an evening dress at a barn dance, and perhaps a temptation to thieves.

They may have scorned my fancy bike, but on the up hill journey from Gilcrux to Bulgill I was able to get well ahead, then whiz down back to them as they wobbled slowly up the steeper inclines. Without the help of gears, it took them twenty minutes to reach their house.

The house was two stories built of moss covered grey stone; it almost merged into the surrounding landscape. Aunt Esme' informed me that it was covered in lichen which only grew in pure country air, that it was more than a hundred years old, and that it had been an inn. I thought to myself, it must have been a humble inn, compared with say, White Horse Close in Edinburgh.

The interior of their house was dark; the small windows restricted the light and the grey stone reflected little. The room was warm; the fire had been smoored to burn slowly. The furniture was simple: a large scrubbed table surrounded by four wooden chairs plus a further two against the wall. There were doors on each side of the fireplace, which was opposite the table; two small windows lit each end of the room. Under the windows at one end of the room there were two wooden sinks—one deep one shallow—both lined with zinc and a metal ringer grip dividing them. Next to the sinks a door opened out to a stone-flagged passageway, leading to a bright sort of outhouse.

The entranceway darkened as a man came down the corridor; he was introduced as Uncle Tom. Uncle Tom looked me in silence, but before this got awkward there was rapping on the door: the carrier had arrived with my case and the railway's Scammel, a three-wheeled vehicle with a flatbed attached. When I signed for the case, I nearly put the qualification contents not examined, but thought better of it.

June was detailed to show me to my room, which was quite large, but coomb-ceiled. It housed a short double bed, an upright wooden chair, a marble-topped washstand topped by a willow pattern basin and ewer. June indicated a matching chamber pot under the bed. She informed me that it was only for peeing in, 'If you need a poop you have to go to the bottom of the garden. Oh! And aim for the side it's less noisy.'

I asked where one got the water to wash? She answered, 'There's water in the jug. When it's empty you fill it up from the pump in the outhouse.'

I washed and changed into a clean shirt, put on a tie and went down to join the family for the evening meal. Uncle Tom gave me a jaundiced look; it was obviously not de rigueur to wear a collar and tie. The Archers theme tune was playing in my head

During the meal that consisted of rabbit stew and large chunks of homemade bread, Uncle Tom quizzed me about school. He was particularly interested in testing my Latin, having me decline nouns and conjugate verbs for him in the future subjunctive.

Aunt Esme' suggested we eat, 'You're not going to catch him out in Latin. He is in a Catholic school.' The way she said the word 'Catholic' made it sound like something catching. I explained that church Latin was different in pronunciation and cadence to school Latin. I gathered from Aunt Esme's look that this was more information than she needed to know. June asked why I was at a Catholic School, 'Your parents aren't Papes?'

'Eat your food girl and be thankful,' Uncle Tom said. I wondered what precisely she was to be thankful for.

'The food is really great,' I said with conviction. Stew as tasty as this boded well for the rest of my stay.

Uncle Tom said, 'We seldom have to buy anything in; we have a big vegetable garden, poultry, lots of rabbits to shoot, and deer too.'

'I have a thriving apiary so we have lots of honey,' said Aunt Esme.

'You're both teachers,' I said. 'What do you teach?'

'General subjects,' said Esme'. 'I am a teaching Head Mistress.'

'I don't teach much,' said Uncle Tom.

'He's a Head Master of a secondary school,' said my Aunt Esme'.

'I make more money from my bees than teaching'.

'Really!'

'I thought it was just a hobby to begin with,' she said.

'We have been successful in holding on to our swarms,' said Uncle Tom.

'When they swarm we have to chase them 'up hill and down dale' as they say. The whole community joins in, even the Vicar' said Aunt Esme'

'Your Vicar sounds quite a character.'

'He's good at lambing and can shear close without drawing blood,' replied Uncle Tom.

'His wife lets the side down,' said Aunt Esme'.

'How?' I asked.

'She hangs the washing out on Sundays,' replied Aunt Esme'.

'As a Head Master even I go to church on Sunday,' said Uncle Tom.

'But you don't, Aunt Esme'?' I said smiling.

'I'm not the Head Mistress of a *local school*' said Aunt Esme' tartly.

'Tom intends to grow mushrooms commercially,' said Aunt Esme'.

I looked across at Uncle Tom. He explained that he first had to make beds (like bunk beds with three tiers) and then make them up with straw and chemical. When the straw and chemical heats up to the correct temperature, we add the mushroom spores. 'This is the tricky bit, if it's too cold they won't take, too hot and they spoil; needs a thermostat for each bed. You're a strong lad; you can help me if you've a mind.' I agreed to help with some enthusiasm.

'On the morrow then,' said Uncle Tom. 'We'd better get the lamps lit meantime!' Uncle Tom lit a row of paraffin lamps, fiddled with and adjusted the wicks, then handed them to each of us to be hung in their appointed places.

We listened to the wireless for a time, but the reception was poor. Aunt Esme` said, 'The accumulator needs to be exchanged next time we are at the garage.'

Uncle Tom drove a 1937 Jowett car which was open—topped and temperamental. It had three gears and required you to double-declutch to change them. He explained that he mainly used the car to go and get the accumulator charged and draw money from the Post Office.

I asked him, 'Why not have them bring the accumulator when they deliver the Paraffin?'

'You should read ergonomics when you go up to 'varsity,' he said. I did not ask him what it meant.

I replied, 'I shall look it up in your dictionary.'

'Ergo, Latin verb to go and gnomic, Greek the science of,' he intoned. It turned out that the word was all Greek.

We soon made our way to bed, each of us picking up a lamp. Uncle Tom informed me about the toilet arrangements with more delicacy than June. The bed was comfortable and I settled down to sleep warmed by the thought that Uncle Tom assumed that I would be going to university.

I awoke in the morning to the sound of the cockerel and the dawn chorus of other birds. I lay in bed until the sun was streaming through the uncurtained window, and there were sounds of activity from the family. I decided to forgo the awkwardness of interrupting some rustic routine.

The W.C was a wooden structure built like a sedan chair, this, June said, was so that it could be moved around the garden to fertilise it all. I asked June why the door opened outwards, she replied, 'To let the daylight in so that you can read.'

'Why does it have three holes in the seat?'

'So that we don't need to queue,' she replied, with a look that said I'd asked a stupid question. I resolved not to join their library group.

I did join the family for breakfast, which was roughly ground oats, to which one could add milk from a large pitcher, plus honey, or in my case salt. The porridge was followed by home—baked bread with mushrooms and eggs fried in butter. There was a large choice of preserves to spread on the bread, greengage, gooseberry, and quince. Aunt Esme's pantry was full of jars from floor to ceiling, all with neat labels denoting contents and date; they were mostly capped with paper frills tied on with string. They did not buy oranges or bananas, but we ate a variety of fruit both fresh and preserved and there were many kinds of pickles and chutneys on offer. Later on in my stay, I observed her sealing her preserving jars by immersing them in the copper boiler normally used for the washing on Mondays.

I had expected to be helping Uncle Tom with his mushroom beds next day, but he declared that it was too good a day for that, so we all got on our bikes and made our way to Allonby to swim. Allonby is on the Solway Firth, has a lovely sandy beach, but is subject to very dangerous tides. We spent many happy days at Allonby but were always careful not to get stranded on sandbanks when the tide raced in. The sand dunes provided privacy for changing and getting dried; June expected her privacy to be respected but did not always return the compliment.

One day we had a visit from the Vicar and his wife. Aunt Esme' ushered them into the parlour: it was a room that I did not know existed. The parlour had a theme of grey and pink down to the last detail. I gathered that it had been in some fashion magazine when they'd been courting. The Vicar was a farmer type and his wife was tall and skinny. I was amused to see that she held Aunt Esme's best china cup with her pinkie sticking out and that Aunt Esme' did likewise. June came in and announced that Mr Grisewood had shown her his big white cock!

'She means his prize Leg-Horne' said Aunt Esme'.

Another day my aunt provided me with a route-map and a packed lunch and urged me to get on my bike and explore the Lake District; this I was happy to do. I found the hills less dramatic than the highlands of Scotland, but better suited to a day's cycle run. The road up through Honister Pass was awesome in its steepness. I took time out to sketch and do some water colour painting. When I got home, the family quizzed me about my trip and wanted to see my attempts to get it down on paper. My uncle remarked on my use of strong dark colours, Aunt Esme'said, 'We would not teach our children to paint like that.'

'It works and it looks good,' said Uncle Tom.

Aunt Esme' asked if she could take the work to show her visiting art teacher. I was quite happy to agree. The art teacher approved my efforts and said that to be an artist; one must gradually depart from the model.

In between the swimming and exploring I spent many hours helping Uncle Tom with his mushroom project. There was one false start, the chemical and

straw failed to heat up to the required temperature. Next attempt was successful and the system produced two crops a day ad infinitum. The two crops of
mushrooms were collected once a day by van and new boxes were left for the
next day's crop. Uncle Tom was delighted and rewarded me generously for my
help in the project. Which was just as well, as June always demanded that I paid
for ice creams or sweets: it was what people in trousers did.

One day Aunt Esme' announced that we must all gather at her apiary to
hunt for wasps' nests, so we walked the hundred yards or so to the field, where
her hives stood in their serried ranks. The wasps were attacking her bees and it
had not been sufficient to cut the means of entrance to just one for the bees to
defend. We came equipped with large cloths and a container of neat carbolic
acid; this was to suffocate the wasps. We found five wasp's nests in the vicinity
of the apiary; one was hanging like a Japanese lantern under the eves of their
outbuildings. I remarked that there were no dead bees or wasps around he
hives. 'Hedgehogs,' said Uncle Tom.

'I don't think I have ever seen a live hedgehog.'

'Well if you do, bring them to our garden, keeps the pests down,' said Uncle
Tom.

'We don't have much trouble with garden pests, we spray the vegetables
with horses pee,' said June.

To change the subject I asked her why bees hum, but no one had the answer
to that.

'Because they don't know the words,' I supplied, there was a collective
groan.

Aunt Esme' said, 'You know if my bees did not collect the nectar from the
clover, it would just evaporate.'

'Yes, and in the process they cross-pollinate the flowers,' I said. 'Did you
know that bee-keeping goes back to the ancient Greeks?'

'Where did you read that?' asked Aunt Esme'.

'In the library in Cockermouth,' I replied. They both glanced at me with
teacher's approval and over to June as if to say, 'follow his lead.'

'What else did you learn?' asked Uncle Tom.

'Well, that the ancient Greeks thought that the biggest bee in the hive was
male, they therefore called it the king and that the bees reproduced without
sex. The Catholic Church took this on board and insisted that all candles used
in holy places must be made of bee's wax because it was made in conditions of
purity. By the reign of Elizabeth the First of England, it was acceptable to
regard the biggest bee as the queen.'

'Quite an impressive research' said Uncle Tom seriously.

'Why do you say Elizabeth the first of England?' Aunt Esme' enquired.

'A simple matter of fact, James the sixth of Scotland succeeded Elizabeth of England. He became James the first of England; which resulted in the Union of the Crowns in 1603.The Union of Parliaments took place one hundred and four years later in 1707.'

'Did you find out any more about bees?' asked Aunt Esme' sharply.

'A little,' I said.

'Well?'

'Oh, the hierarchy, the queen, the workers and the drones; the queen mated with the drones and then they died in the process. The ones that she did not mate with were killed off by the workers at the end of the summer. The worker bees were multi-task. One, they made the wax combs; (octagonal in shape) these were dual purpose as hatcheries for the grubs, which grew into the next generation of worker bees. The other purpose was to store the honey. Two, they collected the nectar to make the honey, some acted as scouts to locate the flowers. Three, they cooled down the hive to keep it at the correct temperature for the queen's egg laying and the grubs hatching. This they did with vigorous use of their wings. Four, they defended the hive against all comers, even unto death (when the bee stings, unlike the wasp, it dies).'

Towards the end of my stay in Cumberland, Aunt Esme' persuaded me to help with the collection of the honey from the hives. The hives were constructed in five levels that fitted one on top of the other, the top one having a pitched roof and covered with roofing felt. We set out, dressed with long coats, our trouser bottoms tucked in to our socks and a wide brimmed hat covered with a net tucked in to the collar of our coats. Aunt Esme' had a purposely made headgear, but it did not stop a bee getting inside in front of her face. Uncle Tom disdained wearing any protection and his arms were bare. We were equipped with sections of hives complete with frames with manufactured wax combs, so that the bees could concentrate their efforts on making honey, to replenish what we were about to take from them. We also carried feather dusters to brush the bees off the combs. The final job was to place the feeders filled with a saturated solution of sugar (The sugar was rationed at the time, but beekeepers were given a special allowance.)

Some of the hives were transported up to the hills, there to gather heather honey, which had more flavour than the clover honey we had harvested. We took the combs to an out-house reserved for the purpose and placed the frames in the extractor after shearing the wax seals of the front of the combs.

We then took turns at cawing the handle of the extractor to create the centrifugal force to draw out the honey.

Suddenly my aunt ordered me to stand very still and keep calm, she and Uncle Tom peeled off the coat I was wearing. Underneath the coat I was completely covered in bees, they opened the windows and the door, then gently brushed the living fur coat off me.

I saw many hedgehogs but became less enamoured with them when I discovered that they were host to lice and even maggots moving between their quills. However the word had gone out that I was interested in hedgehogs so two large ones were handed in on the day before I left for Manchester. They were even lousier than other ones I had seen and stank to high heaven. The whole family came to see me off at Gilcrux station. There was a bit of a 'stushie' because Aunt Esme' had lost my return ticket. A new ticket was bought and I boarded the train complete with a fruit basket containing the two stinky hedgehogs.

Changing trains was more difficult because I had increased luggage. However before the train pulled out from Carlisle, I looked in to see how the hedgehogs were; they appeared to be dead, so I pulled on the leather belt to release it off it's brass stud and lowered the window. Leaning out I handed the basket with the hedgehogs to a porter. The train gathered speed and I waved at the bewildered porter.

My father's partner Eve asked me how I had enjoyed my stay with her sister Esme', and what would I always remember about it.

I answered, 'Bees, mushrooms, and hedgehogs.'

Bus Journey to Work

By Colin McPhail

It was an extremely cold and wet morning when Martin caught the bus as usual from Dalgety Bay to travel to his work in Edinburgh. It was part of his boring ritual every day commuting to work to his office. As usual, having digested the reading of the daily 'Metro' newspaper that recorded all the worst news from yesterday and after his interest had waned on reading the football results, like clockwork he nodded off after the bus picked up more wet and dishevelled passengers from the Park and Ride at Inverkeithing. His slumber came to an abrupt end with a sudden jolt as the bus hit a pothole when it entered central Edinburgh. He then got off at his usual stop in Queensferry Street and thought it was unusual that he was the only one to leave the bus at that stop. Usually there were at least a dozen passengers getting off at that stop. He felt the weather was even colder and windier in Edinburgh than in Fife as he trudged along Princes Street with its columns of slow moving buses travelling in each direction. Everybody that he passed was wrapped up in their winter attire to repel the cold wind and rain. Where he caught a glimpse of their faces they were sullen with a serious stare as if the whole world had descended upon them. They walked and silently crossed over the road junctions seemingly hell bent on their personal missions to where ever they were going. Some of them clutched their briefcases and handbags so tightly it seemed as if they were the most precious possessions they cherished on earth.

He turned into the side road to his office and strode up to the door. Damn, the door was locked! Surely it must be open. He hadn't made a mistake, it wasn't the weekend, it was Thursday but the place was empty. Usually there were 150 people working in the Insurance Company that employed him.

He was aghast to find it closed and decided to go for a cup of coffee in the Waverley Centre. As he sat there pondering and trying to think of a reason for his office being closed he again noticed the people around him. They all looked like zombies with robotic movements, sipping their beverages and munching their food in silence.

After 30 minutes he left to return to his office to see if there had been any change. His office was still closed so he decided to return home and catch the bus back to Fife from its stop in Princes Street. He walked back along Princes Street, the place seemed dead; there was a sudden absence of people, the birds in the Gardens were silent and the columns of buses had disappeared.

He looked across at the Old Town and Castle, a grey mist had descended eerily over them and he shuddered. He had a premonition of something bad happening or of an impending disaster.

He was still walking along outside the shops when suddenly there was a scuffle outside the bank he was nearing and masked men emerged with guns firing back to inside the building. He nervously turned around to see if he was alone. Oh dear! Evidently he was alone in this vast street.

Looking back he could see two private cars approaching at breakneck speed. So much for the vehicle ban. Nonsense, this can't be happening and he collected his thoughts on running away. As he stood there momentarily and hesitated he was spotted by one of the raiders who approached him pointing his gun. He turned and ran but was shot, feeling a searing pain as the bullets tore into his back and legs. He fell heavily onto the pavement with blood oozing out of his back. His thoughts were to crawl away as far as possible and use his mobile phone to ring the police and for an ambulance. He glanced up and down the street. Except for the screeching of brakes and the raiders with their haul jumping into the cars there was still no-one about. He fumbled in his pocket for his mobile and was about to make a call when the raiders, now in their cars, saw that he was still alive. He tried crawling into a shop doorway but before he could get there the cars had mounted the pavement and were speeding towards him. His eyes blinked then closed, as he feared the worst. It's all over, I'm a dead man, they are going to run me over. His body winced when he heard a familiar voice;

'Well, that's the worst pothole we've hit today Martin'. He looked up. I'm alive!

'Wake up Martin, I think this is your stop'.

He looked around, it was his stop and it was still raining, but he was now glowing with the knowledge it had been a fearsome dream and he was rejuvenated for a day's work. He got off the bus laughing to himself as he walked along reflecting over his strange slumber on the bus.

Day of Reckoning

By William Armstrong

'Remarkable!' David Wright, MD, finished rinsing his hands and reached for a paper towel. He eyed the tall slim blonde shrugging into the expensive looking blouse. 'Quite remarkable,' he continued, crumpling the rectangle of tissue and tossing it into the adjacent bin. 'Your general physical condition is superb and your heart would do credit to someone in their forties, not…' the young doctor's voice tailed off in some confusion.

'Not someone in their early sixties,' Hilda Johnson commented tartly, with just a hint of irritation. Damn that old fool, McKendrick. Why did he have to go and die suddenly for anyway. He'd never commented on her youthful appearance. Now she would have to fend off the young doctor's probing questions. She got her temper under control and went smoothly into her routine.

'I suppose it's a combination of several things really. I exercise regularly; jogging mostly, and I also work out at the gym over in Highdale. In addition I eat healthily; a good balanced diet. Plenty of fruit and veg. Then there's Victor…'

Doctor Wright looked up inquiringly.

'He's my dog. An Alsatian, and he requires a lot of exercise.'

'Well,' the young doctor amended Hilda Johnson's file and tossed it into his OUT tray, 'whatever your secret is it certainly works. You haven't been taking any of those new food supplements everybody's raving about?' he queried suddenly.

Hilda Johnson paused in the act of buttoning her costume jacket and smiled. 'No, doctor. Nothing so exciting. It would seem I'm just naturally healthy.' She halted momentarily in the doorway. 'Twelve months time again I suppose?'

Wright nodded. 'I'll leave you to arrange the appointment.'

'Bye then.'

'Bye.' He listened to the sound of her footsteps receding down the corridor. She's very light on her feet he thought, remembering, somewhat guiltily, the long, shapely, sun-tanned legs.

There was a gentle tap and Judy Wilson, his comfortable middle-aged receptionist, put her head round the edge of the door.

The young doctor raised his eyebrows. 'That it then?' he inquired. 'No last minute panics? No broken bones or fainting fits?'

Judy laughed. 'No, nothing like that. And the waiting room's empty. I saw the 'Ice Maiden' leave and thought you might like a cuppa.'

David Wright rose and stretched. 'That's the best news I've had all morning. Tell me,' he queried as they made their way down the corridor to the tiny kitchen cum rest room, 'why the 'Ice Maiden'?'

'Well,' Judy preceded him into the kitchen and busied herself with the teapot. 'She's been widowed now for fifteen years and I've never once heard her name coupled with any man round here.'

Wright stirred his tea thoughtfully. 'Now that does surprise me. She's an extremely attractive woman.' He coloured slightly. 'Didn't you say she's lived here for twenty years? That means she must have been over forty when she arrived in Laxton.'

The stocky receptionist nodded. 'Forty-two to be exact. This was their first home after army life. They seemed happy enough. Then the Major died suddenly. Let's see.' She frowned in concentration. 'This is 1972. That would be back in '57. As you say, she's very attractive. I've heard it put more crudely. All the single men in the district, and a fair number of the married ones, would give their eyeteeth for a night with her. No go though. As far as I'm aware she's never shown the slightest interest in any of them. However, she's very chummy with the lady vicar. There's been a fair amount of speculation about that friendship,' she added darkly.

David Wright frowned. 'You're not suggesting she's a lesbian?' he said incredulously. He recalled the beautiful sun-tanned body, glowing with health and vitality. The perfect breasts. The classic flawless features. 'Surely not. What exactly did her husband die of?'

'The Major?' Judy sipped her tea and searched her memory. 'A heart attack. Very sudden. Of course,' she went on reflectively, 'he always seemed much older than her, though according to their files there was only a couple of years between them. Pity you never met Doctor McKendrick. He could have filled you in on their background. Him and the Major were very close. Played chess every Tuesday night, regular as the clock. My neighbour, Sally Smith, the Johnson's daily, said they left the board set up on a table in the sitting room and you daren't look sideways at it.'

David drained his cup and stood up. 'No family?'

Judy shook her head. 'No. The Major was a very shy man, especially where women were concerned. And she has no time for kids; or men either apparently. Beats me how the two of them ever got together in the first place.'

The young doctor shrugged. 'A lot of strange marriages took place after the war. From all accounts post-war central Europe wasn't the best place to be stranded in.'

'That's true. Mrs Johnson is Austrian. According to Doctor McKendrick she met the Major when she was working as an interpreter with the army. I'd guess she made the running. Maybe she wanted security…who knows.'

'Mm.' Doctor Wright stood for a moment deep in thought, then…'I'll be out on my rounds if anyone calls. See you about one. Bye.'

'Bye.'

Hilda Johnson turned in at the white, slightly sagging gate and made her way her way up a gently sloping path to the vicarage. A low sprawling building, the house exuded an air of genteel neglect, rather like an elderly middle class lady down on her luck. Hilda pressed the ornate bell-push, reflecting wryly as she did so that it could do with a good clean. There was a long pause and then the heavy oak door creaked slowly open. Jean Munro, Laxton's first lady vicar, stood framed in the doorway.

A small plump figure, with chubby features and mousy blonde hair, Jean was usually infectiously happy. This obvious happiness had been instrumental in winning over the small but vociferous minority of parishioners who had opposed her appointment. Now, she was loved by everyone. Today however, she was obviously highly agitated. Traces of tears showed on her normally smiling face.

'Jean, whatever is wrong?' Hilda Johnson stepped forward and put a comforting arm round her friend, drawing her close. A strange, latently sexual thrill pervaded the tall blonde's body as Jean Munro sobbed on her shoulder.

'Oh, Hilda, I'm so glad you're here. Come and see what's happened to the churchyard.' Together they made their way down a long corridor and out through a side door into the vicarage garden. Beyond that was a lych gate which led into a small, well-kept churchyard. Except that today it was anything but neat. Tombstones had been toppled and in some cases smashed. Flower containers had been thrown around and their contents strewn everywhere. Elderly grey-haired Jem Potter, the verger, was forlornly trying to tidy up.

'Who did this?' Hilda Johnson demanded.

'It were that Vince 'Awkins,' old Jem growled angrily. 'I seed 'im an' 'is mates runnin' away when I come past 'ere last night. Told the police I did, an' they said they'd look into it.'

Hilda's heart sank. If Vince Hawkins and his gang were involved it was extremely unlikely that the police inquiries would get anywhere. Everybody in Laxton was afraid of the hulking teenager and his cronies. Any inquiry would be met with a wall of silence. Worse still, his widowed mother, who had been something of a tearaway herself in her young days, would lie through her teeth to provide Vince with an alibi.

'What you need' she said firmly, leading a still sobbing Jean back into the vicarage, 'is a nice cup of tea.'

Several hours later, relaxing in the comfort of her home, Hilda Johnson sipped a glass of wine reflectively and mulled over the events of the day. As far as young Hawkins and his teenage gang were concerned, she doubted if they would ever be brought to justice. The British, she thought sardonically, erred too much on the side of the suspect.

Her mind turned to other things and she frowned, remembering Doctor Wright's probing questions. He doesn't look the type to give up easily, she mused. Still, if British counter intelligence hadn't been able to unearth anything about her past it was unlikely the good doctor would.

Hilda Johnson. She smiled contentedly. The name had a nice ring to it. Much better than Hildegarde Schalke, DP. How she'd hated that abbreviation. She was only one of the millions of Displaced Persons left stranded in central Europe after the war, and it was a chapter in her life she wanted to forget. Now she was Mrs Johnson, a woman of substance, known and respected, if not liked, by the majority of the villagers.

If only they knew the truth. Mrs Hilda Johnson, pillar of the community and Russian sleeper agent. The offer from the Soviet authorities had been too tempting to refuse. Anything to get out of that damned camp. She remembered again the final briefing from her section leader. 'A post as a translator has been found for you in the British zone. You will apply for and obtain this post. It has been arranged. Once settled in you will make yourself known to Major Johnson. It should not be difficult. You have committed his file to memory. He is a quiet scholarly man, unused to women…especially beautiful women. Dress sensibly. No glamour. Your papers show that you are thirty-eight, when in fact you are only twenty-four. The major is forty. Close the gap by being bookish and somewhat reserved. Act accordingly. You should have no trouble. Play him like a fish. Remember, your ultimate goal is marriage and British citizenship.

We know that Major Johnson is leaving the army shortly. He has already been offered a directorship in a large engineering company in the Midlands. If you are successful in your mission you will enter Britain as his wife. Once there, immerse yourself in the British way of life. Become a central figure in the life of the local community. You are a sleeper. It is possible you will never hear from us again. However, if you are called on we will expect an immediate response. The operation could be anything, but a sleeper is very valuable and we will not activate you lightly.

One final point. You are the cutting edge of an operation which has taken many months of careful planning and preparation. Be meticulous in every aspect of your task. Goodbye and good luck.'

The planning and preparation must have been meticulous too, she mused, because everything had gone exactly as planned. And now, here she was, settled into the rural community of Laxton. A known and respected figure in local society.

Life with Michael Johnson had been, after the trauma of post-war Europe, both undemanding and rather pleasant. Their physical relationship had been muted, to say the least. He was very unsure of himself in such matters, while she had realised years ago that her sexual interests lay with her own gender. She'd also realised that such interests would have to be suppressed for the success of her mission.

In those quiet and peaceful years she'd only been activated twice. The first time it had been an innocuous phone call from Hannah Dreschler, a fellow sleeper, saying she would be in the Midlands for a few days and would like to see her again. Hannah, who acted as a buyer for a small but rather exclusive London dress salon, was actually a field agent supervisor. Travelling all over the world as a buyer, she was able to move freely across frontiers, checking on agents everywhere.

'We worked together as translators before I met you,' Hilda had said to Michael over coffee. 'Hannah's very much a career woman. She's made quite a name for herself in dress design. Sells her ideas to the highest bidder. It would be nice to see her again.'

Michael had been delighted. Of course she must have her friend to stay for a few days. Everything had gone perfectly. Slim, dark and bookish, Hannah had captivated the major with her grasp of modern day literature.

Her briefing of Hilda had been much more direct. 'Your mission,' she'd said crisply, 'is to eliminate Georgi Shalakov, a Bulgarian diplomat currently stationed in London. We suspect he is about to defect and this could be embarrassing. He attended the KGB central training school and is familiar with all our latest methods. Take this,' proffering a black and red striped, neatly furled umbrella. 'Shalakov uses public transport regularly. Get behind him and press this stud,' indicating a small chrome button on the handle. 'This will cause a needle to project about a quarter of an inch from the tip of the umbrella. The needle, in reality an extremely neat miniaturised syringe, is loaded with tiny Ricin pellets. Ricin is a drug obtained from the castor oil plant and its toxicity is double that of cobra venom. The mechanism injects the pellet into the victim's leg and the result, so our technical adviser assures me, is death within a day or so.'

After Hannah had gone, Michael had been fulsome in his praise. 'A charming person. We must have her back sometime.'

Hilda had smiled and nodded dutifully, while privately hoping she never saw the lady again.

The assignment had gone perfectly. Hannah had given her a comprehensive rundown on the diplomat's movements, including his route to and from the embassy. Shopping at the autumn sales had provided an excellent excuse for a trip to London. All Hilda had to do was bide her time. A quick jab while behind him at the bus stop, a profuse apology, and the deed was done. Nothing ever appeared in the media, but a week later she received a letter from Hannah saying that their discussion had resulted in a satisfactory conclusion!

For almost a year she'd heard nothing more and then her 'bete noire' had surfaced again. Another letter. Could she visit for a few days? She'd unearthed a valuable book and would like Michael's opinion on it.

Michael was enchanted. 'But of course we must have her again. She can stay as long as she likes.'

Not if I can help it, Hilda had thought grimly.

Initially, Hannah's visit had gone well. She had discussed books at length with Michael. Later she'd taken Hilda aside and outlined the real purpose of her visit. Another mission. 'James Ryan. An extreme left wing politician. In our pay for years and has been a very useful source of information. However, he's had an attack of conscience and is threatening to confess all to MI5. So, take him out. Not the umbrella this time. There have been a couple of failures using that method. Instead, I've been instructed to give you this.' Delving into her capacious handbag she'd produced a slim box with the logo of a famous perfumery on the lid. Opening the box, Hannah had removed a small cylinder, some seven inches long and about an inch in diameter. Six tiny glass ampoules nestled in a padded trough along one side of the container. Arranged similarly along the other side were what appeared to be half-a-dozen fuses. 'Load the fuse in one end; there. Insert the ampoule in the other end and you're all set. Get close to Ryan; this is essential. Press this plunger, so…. It detonates the fuse, which crushes the ampoule and sprays prussic acid into the victim's face. Death by cardiac arrest is instantaneous.' She'd slipped the cylinder into the box and closed the lid.

Hilda's professional training had surfaced. 'It'll have to be done at night. You don't just walk up to a well-known MP without somebody noticing. Then there's my getaway to think about.'

'That shouldn't be a problem,' Hannah had remarked dismissively, rummaging in her bag. 'He's got a flat in one of those big tower blocks. I've got the address some…yes, here we are….' She'd stopped abruptly as Michael entered the room.

'Sorry to barge in like this, girls. Hilda, have you seen my car keys?' Catching sight of the box lying on the table he'd moved closer. 'I say, that's an unusual logo. What is it?'

'Just a present from Hannah,' Hilda had replied smoothly, slipping the box into a drawer. 'It's a local brand of perfume she found in Tel-Aviv.'

'Really. It looked expensive to me.'

'Your keys,' Hilda said hurriedly. 'Try the kitchen dresser. I think I saw them there.'

'Thanks.' Michael had turned to go. 'Hannah, you must tell me about Israel sometime. See you at lunch. Bye.'

A momentary brooding silence had hung between them, then…. 'Do you think…?' Hannah had said slowly.

'No. I know him too well. He accepted my explanation.'

'Maybe…but I suggest you keep the box in a safe place.'

Thankfully, Hannah had departed the following day, but there was something in her attitude as she said goodbye that made Hilda uneasy. A feeling of foreboding had gripped her as she watched the train disappear down the line.

The mission had gone well. Late one evening Hilda had contrived to bump into Ryan in one of the tower block corridors. Holding her breath she'd exploded the ampoule in his face and made good her escape. The media gave the MP's demise front page coverage, and a statement by the police that death was due to heart failure tied everything up nicely. At least, as far as Hilda was concerned.

There had been no more assignments since then, which was just as well, because Michael's sudden death from a heart attack had left her stunned.

He'd gone down to London on business and had collapsed in his hotel. Death must have been virtually instantaneous, according to the examining doctor who had been called. Somehow the whole affair was eerily reminiscent of her last mission. Try as she might, Hilda couldn't rid herself of the feeling that there was more to Michael's death than met the eye.

Although she was now comparatively wealthy, something she'd always craved, Hilda found, somewhat to her surprise, that she missed the tall, gentle ex-soldier. She'd never loved Michael in the true sense of the word, but the years had brought about a deepening tenderness in their relationship.

Well, she mused soberly, slipping into her jogging suit, that was all behind her now. Hopefully there would be no more missions. Calling to Victor she set off on her evening run round the village.

Her routine never varied. Down the main street; past the vicarage and out into the country, the big dog loping effortlessly beside her. Past isolated houses, including the one where Vince Hawkins and his mother lived, and farms where resident dogs barked angrily at the running pair. Turning right at the crossroads, Hilda began the long uphill grind which would take her to the top of Netley Bank, where she could look out over the village. The sun was just dipping behind the western hills and the late spring evening was quite chilly. Ideal running conditions she thought, leaning into the climb.

Victor had stopped and was investigating an interesting scent in the hedgerow. No matter; he'd catch up with one of those electrifying bursts of speed he liked to indulge in every so often. The road ahead levelled off and Hilda relaxed, running easily now. Rounding a bend she was suddenly alerted by the sight of four figures up ahead. Vince Hawkins and his cronies, Roy Smith and the Bentley twins. Trouble, she thought grimly, but I've every right to be here and I don't intend to back down.

The four youths spread across the road and eyed the steadily approaching runner. 'Well, well,' Vince Hawkins muttered, 'if it isn't the 'Ice Maiden' herself, and without that bloody great dog.' Smirking at the others, he stepped sideways into Hilda Johnson's path.

Hilda slowed to a halt, heart pumping steadily, anger clearly visible in her cold grey eyes. 'Let me pass,' she demanded imperiously.

'Why should we?' Vince retorted. 'We've as much right to be here as you have. Isn't that so?' he appealed to the others.

There was an instant chorus of agreement from Roy Smith and the Bentleys. It didn't do to disagree with Vince Hawkins.

Stepping back, Hilda drew a small silver whistle from her pocket and blew it. Victor, I hope you're listening.

The big Alsatian came sweeping round the bend, running low, ears flattened against his skull. In the gathering dusk he looked more wolf-like than ever.

'Stay!' his mistress commanded, as Victor skidded to a halt beside her. His lip lifting in a soundless snarl the Alsatian surveyed the startled quartet.

Red haired Roy Smith was the first to break. 'Look, Missus Johnson,' he began awkwardly, 'we didn't mean no harm. Vince was just kidding.'

'And I suppose,' Hilda retorted with heavy irony, 'you were just kidding when you vandalised the churchyard the other evening?'

Roy shuffled uncomfortably. 'We never meant to…'

'Shut up you bloody fool,' Hawkins shouted angrily.

Barking furiously, Victor lunged at him.

Jumping back from the raging dog, Vince tripped and fell heavily. There were audible sniggers from the Bentley twins.

'That's enough, Victor,' Hilda said crisply. 'The young gentlemen won't bother us again.' Together the tall woman and the big dog faded into the dusk.

Vince Hawkins scrambled to his feet, face contorted with fury. He knew the others were pleased to see him fall. They resented his bullying leadership, but were too scared to do anything about it. 'Damn the stuck-up bitch. I'll get even with her…and her bloody dog. See if I don't.'

'You mean you actually accused Vince Hawkins to his face?' Jean Munro gasped, eyeing her friend in amazement. 'Oh, Hilda, you were taking an awful risk.'

'I doubt it,' Hilda Johnson said confidently. 'Bullies almost always back down and anyway, they were all scared of Victor. Besides, young Smith practically admitted to the damage in the churchyard.'

'Mm.' Jean sipped her tea. 'Victor's your third dog, isn't he?'

'That's right.' The tall woman looked at her friend speculatively. 'You should get a dog yourself. It would be good company for you.'

Jean grimaced. 'Oh, I don't think so. I'd much rather have a cat. Dogs scare me.'

Hilda shrugged. 'Suit yourself. Personally I dislike cats. Victor won't have them in the garden.'

'Anyway' she rose gracefully, 'I must be getting back. See you tomorrow.'

There was no sign of Vince and his cronies when she went out for her evening run. Home again, she turned Victor out into the walled garden, while she had a shower. Vaguely, through the sound of running water, she heard him barking, but when she finished showering all was quiet.

Slipping on her dressing gown, Hilda opened the door and called softly, 'Victor, here boy.' Nothing. She called again, louder this time. Still nothing. A vague sense of uneasiness gripped her. Dressing hurriedly, she went out into the darkness, torch in hand. Down near the gate she saw a dark shape sprawled on the lawn. An icy feeling of foreboding gripped her as she ran down the path.

Victor lay on his side, a crossbow bolt protruding from his left eye socket. 'Oh, Victor,' Hilda sobbed, dropping to her knees; 'what have they done to you?'

Emlyn Jenkins, the local vet, held up the bolt he'd taken from the dead dog's head. 'It lodged in the brain. Death must have been instantaneous. He wouldn't have suffered.'

'And that's supposed to make me feel better?' Hilda demanded furiously.

'Well, no.' The normally cheerful vet was suddenly serious. 'It's just that I hate to think of any animal suffering.'

Constable McLaren, young, smart and enthusiastic, looked up from his notebook. 'Can you think of anyone who might harbour a grudge against you?'

Hilda Johnson paused for a long moment. The germ of an idea was beginning to take shape in her mind. 'No,' she said slowly; 'nobody I can think of.'

'Well,' the young constable shut his notebook with a snap; 'I'll ask around, but I don't hold out much hope. Whoever it was will probably ditch the bow in the river, or some pond. However, I'll check out the local sports shops. We might just get a lead there. Goodnight, Mrs Johnson. I'll see myself out.' The door closed softly behind him.

'He's right of course.' Jenkins rose to his feet. 'Unless he can turn up a lead in one of the sports shops it'll be like looking for a needle in a haystack.' There was a momentary awkward silence.... 'Do you want me to....'

'Dispose of the body? Yes please.'

Much later, Hilda Johnson sat at her kitchen table, a small wooden box open in front of her. She sat for a long time, deep in thought, going over the task she had set herself. Finally, satisfied that the plan would work, Hilda hid the box at the back of her linen cupboard and went to bed.

Rising early next day, she went out on her usual morning run. Striding past the Hawkins' cottage she felt a wave of fury grip her. Gradually, as the run progressed, she got her temper under control. There was no doubt in her mind that Vince had killed Victor, but her revenge had to be carefully planned.

After lunch she called on Jean Munro. The young vicar was shocked to hear of Victor's death. 'It couldn't have been Vince Hawkins, could it?' she said hesitantly.

'No,' Hilda lied smoothly. 'I don't think so. Probably some crank who hated dogs. Anyway, what about yourself? Have you thought any more about getting a pet?'

Jean smiled. 'Yes I have. Old Mrs James is going on holiday and she's asked me to have her cat. If he settles in she says I can keep him. Wouldn't that be wonderful?'

Hilda shrugged. 'I suppose so, though I still think, given that you live alone, you'd be better with a dog.'

Back home, Hilda Johnson got out the small box and checked the contents once more. Carefully, she loaded the cylinder with the small firing charge and the ampoule. Then, slipping the loaded weapon into her jacket pocket, she returned the box and its contents to the cupboard.

It had just crossed her mind that, fifteen years on, the ampoules might have lost some of their potency, when she saw a black and white cat scraping in the back garden. Rage rose in her like a flame. Victor had only been dead a short time and already cats were invading what used to be his territory. The idea flashed into her mind that this would be an ideal opportunity to test the ampoules. Easing the back door open she made her way down the path, the loaded cylinder clutched firmly in her hand.

The cat, a rough-coated tom, stopped scraping and eyed her suspiciously. 'Puss, puss,' Hilda crooned as she advanced. A momentary hesitation, then it moved towards her. Smoothly, arm outstretched, Hilda depressed the plunger and stepped back, holding her breath as she did so.

There was a sudden convulsion and the cat fell over on its side, face already set in the snarling rictus of death. As Hilda Johnson hurried to get a spade she felt a warm glow of satisfaction. Everything was working out as planned. Soon now, she'd have her revenge.

The opportunity wasn't long in coming. The following evening, Hilda was jogging along the river bank path when she saw the familiar hulking figure up ahead. Pausing only to transfer the cylinder into her hand she moved forward confidently.

'Well now.' The same hateful sneering voce assailed her ears. 'If it isn't Mrs high and mighty Johnson herself, and without her dog.' Vince grinned gloatingly. 'Sorry to hear about his...'accident'.'

'You killed him, didn't you?' The cold hatred in the tall woman's voice made Hawkins look at her sharply, suddenly uneasy.

'What if I did?' he demanded truculently. 'You'll never prove it.'

Smoothly, Hilda raised her arm and pointed the loaded cylinder at the startled Vince. There was the faintest 'pop' and the droplets of prussic acid hit his face. Impassively, she watched in stony silence as Hawkins toppled off the riverbank, dead before he hit the water. His body floated slowly out into midstream, and then disappeared beneath the surface.

Arriving home, Hilda packed the cylinder into its box, which she secreted once more in the cupboard. Over a glass of wine she reviewed the whole episode. The killing of Vince Hawkins was dismissed from her mind immediately. Her training had instilled into her a belief that all such 'targets' were expendable. No, all she had to do now was to dispose of the box and its contents. Probably it would be best buried in the garden. At least there would be no prying eyes, wondering what she was up to. Smiling contentedly, Hilda Johnson went upstairs to bed.

Sergeant Gibson scowled at young McLaren. 'I know you couldn't care less about Vince Hawkins, but his old lady's been in saying he didn't come home last night. Ask around. Somebody must have seen him.'

'But Sarge,' the young constable protested; 'it isn't the first time he's disappeared, sometimes for two or three days.'

The big sergeant waved his hand dismissively. 'I know, I know, but go through the motions, otherwise his ma will be on the phone to the Superintendent in Highdale. Oh, and here...' he passed a scribbled note to McLaren. 'You can look into this as well.'

McLaren frowned as he scanned the note. 'Sarge, you must be joking!'

'Just do it. Smith was on nightshift and he said the lady was in tears. So get on with it. Simpson!' Gibson jerked his thumb a lanky constable who had just come in. 'You go with McLaren, he'll fill you in.'

Sitting in the patrol car, McLaren went over the sergeant's instructions.

'Bloody hell,' Simpson swore disgustedly. 'I wonder what Dirty Harry would have made of all this?'

'Dirty Harry?'

'You know. Clint Eastwood in the movie.'

'Oh...yeah. Anyway, let's show willing. We'll make a few calls.'

Hilda Johnson had just opened the box on the kitchen table when the sound of a car engine made her glance through the window. The police car had halted at the gate and PC Andy McLaren was walking briskly up the path.

Hurriedly, Hilda grabbed at the open box. It skidded across the shiny table surface and fell, eluding her vain attempt to catch it. She watched in open-mouthed horror as the ampoules shattered on the floor. The scream welling up in her throat died, stillborn, as the deadly fumes paralysed her system and Hilda Johnson collapsed, her lifeless body sprawling on the tiled floor.

McLaren pressed the bell again. It rang insistently and he waited for sounds of movement. Nothing. Well, he thought sourly, making his way back down the path, it's not vital anyway.

'No luck?' Simpson cocked a speculative eye at his partner.

McLaren shook his head as he adjusted his seatbelt. 'Not in, obviously. Let's try the school. Miss Eaton's keen on pets and she's got the kids thinking the same way. You never know, one of them may just have seen the vicar's cat.'

In the Garden

By David Cruickshanks

Part 1

It was black. The suffocating black of nightmares, when you fight to regain consciousness and wonder if you ever will. The unseen demon is crushing out your life's breath, compressing your chest. You hear first, the straining of your rib cage, then the smaller bones crackling like firewood, and you still grasp at the blackness, clawing, hoping, pleading in silence to reveal the demon's face, yet terrified of the horror that you might uncover and then you are pinned back again, your heart is trying to break through the prison of your rib cage as the bigger bones bend and strain and then, like a beaten oak tree in a storm you hear the gun-shot crack of bone and the hiss of a lung leaking blood and precious air and you sink deeper and deeper knowing that only waking up will save you.

Khalid screamed out. He bicycled his legs at the pitch black air. His hands fought off imaginary monsters before his eyes grew accustomed to his surroundings. He breathed in rasping sobs, tasting the salt from his own sweat and shivering with the chill on his back as the drenched shirt, once respectably white, steamed on his heaving torso.

He fumbled for the small oil lamp and lit the tallow. The scratched brown earth flickered and danced a macabre jig around him, illuminating the suffocating gloom. He was still in the bunker.

He looked around for something human and caught sight of a photograph he had snatched when the shells started falling. He scraped some loose earth from the glass, revealing the smiling ghosts in stilted poses, behind them, the looming frontage of the Coliseum. A tear fell on the glass and he smiled and remembered a time before this.

Naliah and Ahmed had been their neighbours for almost a month. As one of the town's most popular and senior doctors, Khalid had first met them when they registered at his practice on the outskirts of their large confident suburb.

Khalid and his wife Zara welcomed them into their neighbourhood. Zara fussed over the young woman, teaching Naliah how to make sweets bread and lemonade, using the lemons from her precious garden. Zara had a sideline, selling lemonade to a stall holder in the nearby market. Every Friday, before prayers, a battered lorry would turn up and a wizened old man and a wide-eyed boy collected several churns of concentrate for carbonating. Naliah loved Zara's lemon grove and helped with the pressing and mixing. At sunset they would sit in the garden, sucking in whatever breeze there was, drinking tea with lemon and chatting about this and that.

'Is Ahmed settling in alright?'

'Oh yes Zara, he has always loved tinkering with cars and now that he is own boss with his own garage we are able to afford the finer things in life.'

Zara replied 'Oh yes, the finer things in life, like a bigger mortgage.'

Zara's hearty laugh drowned out the rustling branches. She spoke again aware of the uncomfortable silence.

'I just hope you haven't stretched yourself to live here, so many young couples struggle just to show how well they are doing, Khalid and I we started off small, we didn't even have a coloured TV, now everyone has satellite dishes. Zara looked up to the sky and received chastisement from an imaginary god before turning her face toward Naliah. 'Oh god listen to me, no wonder you are smiling, I must sound like my mother.'

'Don't worry about us Zara, my father gave us some money for the business when we married and Ahmed is planning to upgrade the garage, honestly some of the stuff he is using is falling to bits.'

'And what about babies, when they come along, Naliah, how will it be then?'

Naliah smiled. 'I don't know Zara, let's hope people's cars keep on breaking down.'

"Anyway where are your babies Zara?'

Zara's eyes clouded over, she turned away from Naliah and looked over at the trees, her hand swept an arc over the lemon grove.

"I have all this what do I want with a child?'

Naliah took Zara's hands in hers.

'I'm sorry I didn't mean to pry.'

Zara cut in with a raised hand.

'Let's go down and chat up the men, maybe they will let us join their philo-sophical discussion that is bound to be oh so important.'

Khalid and Ahmed sat at the bottom of the lemon grove, the smoke from their cigarettes snaking upwards as the wind shivered the lemon trees in the dying gloom.

'I was hearing on the radio last night that things are not so good between us and the Americans,' said Ahmed.

'I haven't known it any other way.' replied Khalid, using his hand like a paintbrush to chase away the smoke. He leaned towards Ahmed, noting the worry lines on the young man's forehead.

'I know what you are saying Khalid, my father says the same things but all the same, the radio said that an invasion was closer now than ever.' Ahmed's eyes widened as if he had just caught sight of the American forces cresting the hills overlooking Khalid's house. He uncrossed his legs and stamped out the cigarette on the moist earth.

Khalid drew back and sighed, his arms folding as he let out a stale bag of air.

'Ten years ago, we all felt the same, the radio told us that we had to get our-selves ready, store water and food the ministry said, they even told us to make bomb shelters and in they end what happened, nothing that's what, all that worry and anxiety for nothing. I almost ran out of Prozac there was so much panic around the town. The bloody media, they're always starting a stampede. Anyway, it will be the same this time Ahmed, and if it's not, well you know where to come for some medication if you're stressed out.'

'Thanks Khalid, but I think I'll stick with herbal tea.'

'I wish my patients would do the same, bunch of bloody junkies most of them, anyway listen to me rabbiting on, how's the garage business?'

'Apart from everyone wanting it for nothing, you know Khalid, people just don't know the cost of things anymore. I'm cutting corners a bit just to break even. I'm going to ask Naliah's father for a top up, just for some new equip-ment then we'll be sorted.'

'What are you two conspiring against this time?' demanded Zara, kicking up the dust around the two men.

'Oh, you know Zara, the usual, world domination, the cost of motoring, junkies,' replied Khalid.

'Not to mention disobedient wives, the weather and the state of the football team' said Ahmed, warming up.

'Please! you don't know the half of it,' replied Zara, an index finger now lev-elled at her husband, why don't you stay home and work in the house for a week and I'll go and prescribe painkillers for all your old lady friends at the clinic and we'll see who's complaining on Friday. Oh and Ahmed, don't take your cue from this grump otherwise you'll be grey and wrinkled by this time next year.'

Before Ahmed could fight his corner Zara had interrupted him. 'Right, let's get some lemons in before dark, it's too hot to pick them tomorrow and we'll all die of thirst.'

'Is my wife right Naliah? Will we all die of thirst if the lemons are not picked?'

Naliah, who had been engrossed in the theatrical exchange between husband and wife looked up at the doctor.

'I don't think so Khalid, Zara and I have enough lemons for a weeks supply of lemonade.'

Khalid looked up at the source of the soft voice, meeting her eyes for a second and then staying a second longer. The corners of her mouth turned upwards before she turned away.

The doctor cleared a sudden dryness in his throat;'Come on Ahmed, let's get the ladders and leave these two to their womanly pursuits.' mocked Khalid.

That night Khalid had a strange dream, a young woman with her arms outstretched and her face smudged with tears loomed over him, her body rocking with sobs. Her face was a blur to him but he recognised the soft voice and the smell, the smell was unmistakable. He woke sweating and shaking. He got up and tiptoed down the stairs and into the garden. He sat down on the bench where Naliah and his wife had teased him earlier.

The stars blinked through the leaves of the giant Cedar in the middle of the lemon grove.

Khalid fumbled for a cigarette and gazed across at the shimmering lights in the foothills, he looked over to where Ahmed and Naliah would be sleeping.

'What's the matter?' asked Zara, propping herself up with her pillow. 'Did you see a ghost?'

Khalid stood at the bedroom door, his moonlit face frowning. 'Not exactly.' His hesitant reply barely audible.

'Come back to bed, I'll change the sheets in the morning, they are so sticky, we can talk about it tomorrow.'

'There's nothing to talk about, I just had a nightmare that's all, go back to sleep Zara.'

He moved towards his side of the bed and pulled back the damp sheet, the reflection from the moon bathing him in soft blue light. He climbed back into bed and stared at the ceiling.

'It was one of your patients wasn't it?'

'I hope not, go to sleep Zara.'

The next day Khalid was pacing around the kitchen, his large handsome face folded into a frown.

'My shirt has a stain Zara, look!' he pointed like a boy that had just seen his first Elephant at the zoo.

Zara watched him as he sat fiddling with a bowl of dried fruit and figs.

'You must have spilled some breakfast on it, anyway why are you in such a foul mood?'

Khalid's anger subsided, he hated it when she was so direct.

'It's just that I like a clean shirt, that's all.' He muttered, diagnosing the stain with his doctor's eyes, hoping that if he stared long and hard enough it would disappear.

'By six o'clock tonight that stain will have plenty of others for company, you can join the dots before you put it in the washing machine.'

'Why do you make fun of everything Zara?'

'Look Khalid, it's just a stain, it'll wash out.'

She took Khalid's hands and leaned into his face, her eyes scanning his worry lines.

'Is there something else.'

He shook his head. 'I'm fine really, perhaps I've been working too hard.'

She kissed him on the forehead and he wrinkled his nose and turned away.

'Tonight at least your sheets will be clean.'

'You are indeed a dutiful wife.' he laughed, the wrinkles around his coal black eyes creasing up.

'Can you tell Naliah, I will see her in an hour, we are going shopping.'

He turned back towards her. His right hand on the door handle, battered leather case straining his left shoulder socket.

'Careful Zara, you know they are struggling.'

'I know Khalid, but we girls must have some retail therapy, we'll just do a bit of window shopping don't worry your credit cards will survive.'

'I'll see you tonight.'

That morning the heat was unbearable. The dawn's blue sky, now baked white by the mid morning sun, had long been deserted by migrating clouds. The parched earth wrinkled and shrivelled like the old lemonade seller.

In the lemon grove Zara and Naliah churned gallons of lemony liquid. They pumped water from the well, their clothes matted with sweat.

Zara stretched out her back, arching her face to the relentless sun, her free hand shielding her eyes from the fierce heat.

Nahlia was bent double, struggling with a stubborn churn which tore great lumps out of the caked earth as it was dragged against its will.

'Right Nahlia, let's leave this to the men, it's too hot, I'm ready to pass out. Let's get changed and have a bit of lunch.'

'Thank the prophet Muhammad, peace be upon him. My back is crying out for a sit down and some tea.'

Khalid drove the two miles each day to his surgery; within a mile the landscape of large stone mansions gave way to corrugated shacks. Like most days Khalid shared his journey with Ahmed, dropping him off at his garage a few hundred yards from the surgery. The corrugated tin structure which housed a motley lamp, rusted welding gear and an assortment of worn tools, swayed in the slightest breeze. Inside, Ahmed's assistant was already prising a reluctant exhaust from it's mounting.

'I can pick you up at six o'clock,' shouted Khalid above the din of a hammer. The exhaust was putting up a good fight.

'See you then, and I'll take a look at your car as well, it isn't sounding too good, timing's out I think.'

'Leave it for another day, and Ahmed?'

'Oh no, I feel a lecture coming on doc.' He smiled

'Too late, it's coming anyway, take it easy, you need a rest. I've been watching you recently, you're worn out.'

'I'll be fine, see you at six, and Khalid, stop worrying.'

Zara had just finished showering when the phone rang. Her long dark hair clung to the receiver. It was Khalid.

'You better get Naliah, there's been an accident.'

There was a few seconds of silence.

'Zara, are you there?'

'Yes, yes, is it Ahmed, how bad is he?' The receiver shook as she spoke. 'Tell me Khalid, I need to know what I am dealing with when I talk to her.'

'It's bad, his chest has been crushed by that bloody ramp. I told him to take it easy but he wouldn't listen, said the ramp would be good for a few months.'

'Where is he? What are you going to do.'

'I'm at the hospital now, he is in the operating theatre. I couldn't do much for him at the garage.'

'You saw him? What was he like?'

'Pale as death, if that's what you mean,' replied Khalid.

'I couldn't do much for him at the garage, one of his lungs had collapsed and I couldn't even give him Morphine.'

'I'll get Naliah and we'll get there as soon as we can.'

'No, hang on, I can do nothing here. I'll pick you up. The other doctors can take care of my home visits, I'll see you in fifteen minutes.'

She put down the receiver and pressed the tips of her fingers hard against her lips. She heard a knock at the door and said a silent prayer.

Khalid watched Naliah's bowed head as she sat in the A and E waiting room. Her shoulders undulating as she struggled to control her sobbing. He breathed in her odour of sweat and lemons and sighed. Her once olive face almost transparent now and smudged by tell tale tear tracks. Tiny wisps of hair escaped from her head scarf. Her tiny hands mangled the life out of a handkerchief. He wished he could take her hands in his.

Zara was speaking softly to her. Her hands, wrinkled by the pressing of lemons rested on Naliah's wrists. Her words of comfort swallowed up in the ether of the waiting room. They waited under the sick green light of the hospital. Hours went by yet Naliah never moved. Zara had offered to get some tea but Khalid insisted that he went. They drank in silence. In the late afternoon a young doctor approached them.

'Mrs Hussain?'

'Yes' Naliah stood up as if ordered, she nearly fell over and Khalid put an arm out to steady her. 'How is he? Please tell me he is going to be okay.'

Khalid noticed her eyes, bloodshot and tear stained, her hands still strangling the tiny handkerchief ball. Zara looked at him, her eyes locked onto his and he looked away. The doctor stood in his coat, which dwarfed him, his thick stubble had taken root from the previous night as he fought to save lives in between cups of strong black coffee and the odd nap. In what Khalid thought was a Herculean effort the young consultant lifted his head and stared straight at Naliah.

'I am afraid that I can do nothing more for him. Both his lungs are crushed beyond repair, they are filling up with fluid, he is struggling to breathe, even with a ventilator, I have to tell you that he will not last the night.'

'That's nonsense, tell him Khalid, you are a senior doctor, tell him. Ahmed is young, he's only twenty-five, he can survive, he is strong, tell him Khalid, tell him.'

'This man is a specialist Naliah, what he says is true we must go home now.'

'I want him home with me.'

'It is impossible Naliah' said Zara, squeezing Nahlia's tiny hands.

Nahlia twisted away from Zara wrenching her hands free. Her eyes narrowed at Zara who caught unawares jumped back.

'I want my husband home!'

The hospital receptionist raised her head above the admissions book and several walking wounded turned to look at them.

'I want my husband home,' repeated Naliah.

The young consultant sighed and looked at Khalid.

'It is possible, if you were to administer treatment at his bedside I would be willing to make an exception.'

'Are you sure?' quizzed Khalid, 'I don't want to risk reprisals.'

'Do it Khalid!' said Zara, 'take him home.'

At four o'clock in the morning Ahmed stopped breathing, just as darkness gave up it's hold. Khalid watched Naliah as she sat hunched on the chair next to the bed. The room smelled of damp dead moths. Khalid could only see the back of her body like a bundle of rags. She convulsed with sobbing, the sound was muffled as her hands covered her mouth, stemming the flow of grief, building it up for another time. He moved around and sensing him she looked up…he took her hands and held them in his sweating palms.

'Naliah, you must rest now, there is nothing we can do until morning, please take the sedative.'

He motioned with his eyes to the glass by Ahmed's bedside table and the single white pill on it's cracked vanished surface.

'Ah yes Dr Khan, the magic pill. Will it bring Ahmed back? Why could you not save him, you were there, in the garage, you could have saved him, you're supposed to be the best there is. The high and mighty but oh so congenial G.P.'

Khalid flinched as he caught sight of the red weals around her swollen eyes. The cracked skin around her nostrils burned raw in the glow from the bedside lamp.

He turned to look at the pale grey body. A few hours earlier his contorted face pleaded with Khalid to give him a merciful death. His body contorted with strain of breathing. Khalid administered enough morphine to stem the pain, perhaps more.

Now Ahmed's supine body cast a shadow as the daylight leaked through a crack in the shutters.

Naliah was silent also.

'I must be going now Naliah, there are things to be done. 'I will ask Zara to come over and make some tea.'

Khalid spoke softly, he had spoken these words with bereaved families many times over, yet this one was different. Tears welled up in his eyes. He thought of Zara, at home, alone and waiting for news. Then he looked at the pathetic little bundle who had cried herself silent.

'I will go now, but I'll get Zara to come.'

Nahlia stood up and placed her hand onto his chin, his salt tears leaked a path onto the back of her wrists.

'I am so sorry Khalid,' she said, shaking her head from side to side. 'Please forgive me.'

She pushed her face up close to his, her lips meeting his salty like limpets on a rock, they clung to each other as Ahmed's skin turned blue.

Khalid pushed Naliah away and stared at the corpse.

'I need to go,' he stuttered, picking up his bag, the contents falling to the floor, he looked to Ahmed expecting him to react to the noise of the scattered pill bottles.

'No Khalid, I'm sorry I didn't mean to.' whimpered Naliah, she followed him around the room then bent down to pick up the pills.

Nahlia, listen to me, it's not your fault, the truth is I wanted to hold you, but it's impossible you can see that can't you.'

Naliah's eyes narrowed, her lips, once full and red, now tight like the mouth of a shell.

'You arrogant bastard Khalid, you think that you made it all happen, that you make everything happen and then you think you can stop it by snapping your fingers and everything goes back to normal.'

'Naliah, let's leave this now, I have to go back to Zara.'

'Run away Khalid, run to your precious Zara, and pray she never hears about this.'

Part 2

Khalid's neighbours laughed when they saw him trundling backwards and forwards, his wheelbarrow laden with pick and shovel. At times he questioned his own sanity. After Zara left he lost his sense of purpose. Together they loved this garden. The breath giving aroma of lemon trees that bounced the light this way and that. Together they loved the crisp branches which tamed the searing sun at summer's height, providing shelter from its damaging rays. A huge stern Cedar commanded the centre, its branches fanned out in a giant protective circle around which the lemon trees cooled and bowed in the wind as if paying homage to their sentinel.

When she left him, the lemons went unharvested. They bobbed up and down on their burdened branches while he embedded himself in his sagging leather armchair. The television babbled and fizzed in the corner of his decrepit sitting room. Adverts for washing up liquid and soft drinks passed by in a blur, unable to register his guilt ridden conscience. As the days passed the television gave up in a half hearted explosion. If it wasn't for the wind up radio on his dusty sideboard he would never have begun the project.

He hacked away at the hard earth, first with the pick. Back breaking work. Sweat rolled down his black matted forehead, soaking his thick head of curly hair. His hair was what Zara had loved most about him.

Her image flashed before him. Perhaps she too would think he was mad. Her brown eyes narrowing in consternation. 'Always day dreaming Khalid' he could hear her say. Like that time when they visited Europe. Khalid was mesmerised by the architecture; the sand blasted marble Piazzas of Milan, the Gothic splendour of the Notre Dame. He desperately wanted to visit London but Zara was anxious to return home.

'You've had enough of western culture, it's time to go home, I have a business to run, the lemons won't harvest themselves,' she said, her index finger pointing up at his chin. She raised her eyes up to his and smiled, then her face softened.

'You will come to London one day.'

His body ached with the effort of digging. Every muscle in his back jarred into action after years of wasting away. His lungs worked hard. He coughed and cleared dust from his throat. As the days went by curiosity from the neighbours grew.

'We thought you were dead, Khalid.' shouted Basira, over the garden fence one scorching afternoon. 'My son was at the surgery yesterday and they told him that you had taken some leave, nothing the matter is there?'

'As if you cared' he hissed under his breath.

'What are you doing there?'

'Oh just a little project of mine Basira, something Zara always wanted.'

'Where is Zara these days, you haven't buried her in there have you?'

'Her mother isn't well; she is taking some medicines to her, I imagine she will be gone for a few weeks at most.'

'That's funny I haven't seen her in a month.' Basira queried, her eyes narrowing, her nose seemed pointier than usual.

'I'm sure it isn't as long as that, anyway I must smooth out this concrete before it dries out.'

'Looks like a bunker, you're not taking the news seriously are you?'

'No' replied Khalid, 'just a storehouse for the lemons. This global warming is spoiling them.' He smiled at Basira, ashamed and impressed by his ability to lie so easily. He would have to think up a better story tomorrow.

The next morning was the hardest of his life. But Ahmed's words about the American troops had stuck in his mind. He thought back to Ahmed on his death bed, then the kiss with Naliah and the sequence of events that led to Zara racing out of the house with only a tiny black suitcase and him nursing a bruised cheek.

He looked up at the lemon trees, then he knelt down and prayed. After a few minutes he stood up.

The sabre swathed the still air.

Sinewy branches floated down, down, down to the dusty earth.

The soft lemons landed with a thud.

He cried bitter tears.

The giant Cedar loomed silently over the carnage.

The project was taking shape.

Another week went by. The wind-up radio reported an escalation of hostilities. The Americans massed on the border, threatening a full-scale invasion. There had been talk of them using gas or even nuclear weapons but most commentators played down suggestions stating that the Americans were not barbarians.

Khalid accelerated his project now. The neighbours watched with with suspicion and jealousy as he trundled bottles of water and tins of food down the ramp and into the trench. He manhandled the makeshift stove down the ramp in darkness to avoid inquisitive eyes.

One night his concrete mixer had stirred up those next door as he worked under the lazy light of an old oil lamp.

'Quit that noise Khalid, we are trying to sleep.'

'Nearly finished now Mrs Jazeera, won't be long now,' he replied, looking up at the squinting face of his old neighbour in the half-light as she leaned out of the window, a withered hand fanned her in the stifling heat.

That same night another face peered out at him, he caught her piercing eyes looking at him before she ducked into the darkness, her soft warm skin retreating into the cool of her bedroom. He wanted to knock on her door, to confront her as to why she had remained silent, but the truth was that he wanted to kiss her again the night of Ahmed's death. He had only dragged himself back from the brink because his conscience won the battle over his instinct.

Two days later the ground shook. He grabbed the wedding photograph from the dusty sideboard and ran into the garden. Above him a huge black cloud suffocated the sun. Under the giant Cedar he turned a full circle, surrounded by the fallen lemon trees, he clutched at the photograph. He could hear screaming and the cry of a baby. Tears welled in his eyes. Then he heard his name being called and he thought he must be dreaming again, but this time it wasn't Zara.

Naliah was running towards him, her arms outstretched, her beautiful face contorted into a mask of pain.

'Khalid, don't leave me here, take me with you, I'll die out here, please Khalid, pleeeease!'

He had seen her cry before but this time he shut her out. He couldn't look her in the eye, knowing his weakness would make him take her. She clutched his tanned forearms with her little hands, he remembered her clutching the worn out handkerchief at the hospital. More explosions, this time closer. He turned away, wrenching himself free, he ran down the ramp and into the shelter. He fumbled with the bolt mechanism, his hands shaking. He sealed the entrance, his heart thudding hard in his chest. Sweat dripped from his forehead, he fought for breath before his heart jumped again when a thud thud came from the outside of the door. He heard her muffled screams, the thuds from her tiny brown knuckles made him jump. Her screaming, at first frenzied, was reduced to sobs and after two hours, nothing.

He shuddered from the vibrations as the earth began to fracture under the shock of the homing warheads. Khalid trembled and recited prayers. A pot juddered and fell from his makeshift stove, spilling the contents onto the concrete floor of the bunker. Earth began to seep through the wooden joists as they creaked and groaned with the pressure of bombing. He stared, paralysed at the sealed-up door.

The radio announcer belatedly confirmed his worst fears. The Americans had unleashed their shock and awe. People were ordered to take cover, then the radio crackled and then, there was nothing. His single lightbulb popped and he trembled in the darkness.

A month went by in eerie silence. After the initial bombardment which Khalid reckoned had lasted only a few terrifying hours, all was still. He sat, imprisoned, surrounded by emergency provisions. The wind-up radio conspired with the silence. His make-shift stove, provided some heat and the lightbulb had been replaced with a spare. After two weeks the electricity ceased and he lit his first candle. One day he heard scratching at the sealed entrance. Rats he told himself, dirty parasites looking for fresh meat, they would have to wait.

He devised a routine. His primitive chemical toilet had to be prepared daily. He grooved lines in the concrete with an old wood chisel to mark the start of what he thought was morning. The watch he bought in Milan ticked away the hours, reflecting Khalid's face, glowing orange by candlelight. He thought about writing a diary but who would read it?

He restricted himself to one meal a day, reckoning that one gas bottle would last three months. The minimum time he had to stay in the bunker before venturing into the radiation. He knew that six months would give him a better chance of survival and anyway cold food wasn't so bad. He had enough provisions for about eight months.

All this time he bottled up his feelings. He tried not to think of Naliah but she came to him in nightmares. He could see her pleading with him to let her in. He slammed the thick metal door on her only to see her tiny hands snaking through the lead lining, grabbing his throat and tightening. He grappled with her but her grip was fierce. He could feel himself losing consciousness before he jerked awake. Sometimes he woke before her hands grabbed his throat, sometimes he saw her screaming face other times he saw a different face.

'How could you do this to me Khalid? Have I not been a loyal and compassionate wife? Did I not listen to you and give you understanding? Tell me Khalid, please, how did I fail you Khalid, please, I must know.'

His body jerked up in the darkness, he screamed and yelled, fighting the imaginary demon. His body dripping with sweat though the night was ice cold. His chest racked as he forced stale air in and out of his dust infested lungs. He fumbled for some matches to escape the dark. When the candle illuminated the bunker he found himself back in his living nightmare.

Each time he slept he faced the same traumas. He began to fight sleep, afraid of the accusing Zara, afraid of the Naliah who wanted to kill him. He forced himself to think of his childhood and his lemon trees but the thoughts of the lemons brought back the pain of remembering. He thought of the world outside but could not imagined only death and destruction beyond the lead seal.

His eyes welled with tears as he fought to consider a future out of the bunker.

And then it was set. This night he told himself to fear sleep no more. He made a point of tidying the bunker. Everything in its place. He prepared the chemical toilet though he didn't expect to use it. He cleaned the filters through which musty air was pumped and afterwards prepared himself some rice and beans over the stove. The gas bottle he calculated would be two thirds full.

He clutched the wedding photograph, apologised to Zara for spitting on it and wiped it clean with his shirt. Her smile flickered in the weakening light. He held it close to him, the cracked glass cooled his cheek. He traced a callused finger around the line of her cheek bones and smiled, while tears ran down his face. He blew out the candle, lay down on his mat still clutching the photograph. The gas from the pierced bottled snaked into the blacked out bunker.

'The lemon trees are gone Zara, there is nothing here for me now, perhaps, god willing, I will see you soon.' He breathed deeply. His thoughts softened and he became drowsy and content. He could hear his heart thrumming in his ears before it was replaced by a scratching sound and prayed that he would lose consciousness before the rats gnawed over his body. The scratching grew louder, they must be here already he thought, let them choke on every bone he laughed to himself, unable now to feel fear. His mind drifted to Zara, he hoped that she had forgiven him and he could be at peace.

The black cloak of unconsciousness enveloped him and his breathing slowed. His hands flopped from his chest. The photograph remained, the frame rising and falling with the rhythm of his languid breaths.

The scratching had stopped, but he could just make out something much stonger replacing it. There was a loud thudding as the pressure equalised in his ears. Then the sound of metal being scraped against metal. A hiss of dead air escaped and he thought this must be it, my last breath and then a piercing white light invaded his consciousness.

'Khalid?'

This was it, the moment I meet my maker. He thought.

'Khalid, Khalid!'

My god, the prophet Muhammad, peace be upon him is coming for me.

He thought he recognised the soft voice, and he tried to speak but his popping ears revealed a much stronger voice.

"Khalid, it is me Zara."

He winced as he tried to sit up. The damp mud had stiffened his back and he fell backwards. Two firm hands grabbed at his bony fingers, hauling him upwards so that he sat up facing her.

'I'm sorry, I never…' he struggled to find the words, his heart pounded as the cleaner air forced toxins out of his blood stream.

'Here, drink this, you can talk later, we have plenty of time.'

The water tickled his mouth, seeping into the cracks of his lips. He pushed the bottle away and placed the palm of his hand in front of her.

'It never happened you know, I would never do that to you.'

'I know, Khalid.'

'How do you know?' he spluttered, the water forcing his throat to expand.

'I met Naliah, in the mountains. I went there when the bombs came. She took your car, I recognised it. We were forced to shelter together, after all when bombs are falling you cannot be fussy.'

He smiled and tried to open his eyes but the light forced them shut.

'Anyway, Khalid after a week she told me what had happened, that in a moment of madness she had kissed you.'

'Did she tell you it was on Ahmed's deathbed?'

'Yes Khalid, she told me, but she also told me that she wanted to take it further and when you rejected her she decided to tell me that you had raped her. Why I did not believe you I still do not know.'

'Perhaps you do not know me well enough.'

'I know you well enough to know that you would have survived the bombing.'

'Why did it take you so long to return?'

'We were afraid in case the Americans had occupied the city, but in the end the never came after all there's no oil in this part of town.'

'I am sorry about the lemon trees.'

'There will be others, there were no nuclear bombs after all. The soil is not contaminated, we can start again?'

'And Naliah, where is she?' His eyelids strained to open but his vision was blurred, what happened to her?'

He looked up to see the outline of another face but this time the ghostly apparition solidified as his sight restored, he saw another face, smaller and rounder than Zara's. Her soft brown eyes forced him to focus. She was smiling through tears.

'I am here Dr Khan.'

Christmas leave in Gloucester

By Allan Moore

Angus went by train to Ashchurch in Gloucester. During the time he had been away, his father had bought a hotel called Northway House Hotel between Tewksbury and Cheltenham. Angus was surprised that his father, Eve and John were waiting on the platform to greet him.

Eve said, 'Home is the sailor, home from the sea.'

Angus said, 'Yes, a stone frigate in the middle of the Yorkshire moors. The only ships I've been on were the obligatory visit to Nelson's Victory in Portsmouth and, by way of contrast, a modern aircraft carrier HMS Indefatigable.'

The whole family got into the car and drove to the hotel. Northway House was a beautiful Georgian country house that had lain derelict for many years and was now a comfortable place to stay for many permanent guests and people who met there to celebrate family occasions, where the numbers were too many to enjoy in individual houses. One family met every year for Christmas, coming from the many regions of the country that they had scattered to.

Angus observed his father in a new light, in this very different setting from his role as general manager of a large firm employing hundreds of people. Angus watched his father carry out many tasks that he had previously delegated to the managers of the hotels, bars and a variety of catering establishments, which he presided over subject to a board of directors

This was the first time in his father's life that he was running his own business. As the proprietor he would play 'mine' host at one of the bars, work part of the day with the chef, turn his hand to any of the many jobs involved in running a hotel, and was enjoying every minute of it.

Angus found that there were times that his father would find time to relax and chat to him, telling him stories of his own days in the navy from 1914 to 1929. Apart from accounts of his service in the Great War, he had been a cabin boy on a coaster which plied its trade from the Thames up the North Sea coast. Angus quoted the last lines from the poem Quinquierem of Nineveh:

> *Dirty British Coaster with a salt-caked smokestack butting through the channel in the mad March days with a cargo of Tyne coal, pig iron and cheap tin trays.*

His father raised an eyebrow, 'Better not spout that sort of thing on the mess-deck, they might get wrong ideas about you.'

The time that his father had served after the Armistice was interesting to Angus. His father had been one of the complements of three ships sent to found the New Zealand navy. He spent three years there and had he not been married would have transferred to the New Zealand navy when this was offered.

During one of his chats with his father, Angus told him of a curious incident that had recently occurred. Angus had gone ashore from HMS Ceres to Wetherby, the nearest town. When he alighted from the bus, an elderly gentleman asked him for directions to the Angel Hotel. Angus found himself giving directions. The man tipped his hat, thanked him, and set off. Angus was concerned because he had never been to the town before. He followed the directions he had given, and found himself at the Angel Hotel. Angus' father was quite dismissive about this account, probably had a logical explanation said he, but did not offer one.

Angus experienced another strange event. One night as he was climbing up to the attic floor of the hotel and came level with the landing, he saw a monk, not an ethereal ghostly figure but a very substantial one. Angus felt no fear, the monk seemed very benign, he raised his hand in a blessing, turned and moved down the corridor and vanished. Angus did not feel inclined to tell his father, but three days later, a chambermaid came screaming into the kitchen shouting that she had seen the monk. Angus looked at his father,

'There's a rumour that this place is haunted. I don't discourage it, it might attract more business,' said his father.

Angus gave his account of his encounter with monk while his father listened intently and questioned him in detail. Then he was called away. Two days later, his father brought up the subject of the monk.

'Son, you are on leave and have time on your hands. Why don't you take a jaunt to Tewkesbury and find out about the myths and legends of this area?'

Angus went to Tewkesbury and his first port of call was The Hop Pole, an inn once frequented by Charles Dickens. The bar was empty. Angus ordered a glass of cider.

'We don't get many sailors in here,' remarked the elderly man behind the bar.

'I doubt if there would be enough depth in the river to sail a war-ship up here,' replied Angus.

'Where you lodging?' asked the man who was busy polishing glasses.

'Northway House' replied Angus.

'That place is haunted,' stated the man with firm conviction.

'Oh really' said Angus. 'Tell me more.'

'Well, the house was direlict for many years and people saw monks walking along the roofline at dead of night,' he said in a sepulchral voice.

Angus tried to get further information but it was obvious that the man had no more to give.

'Perhaps, you should talk to our librarian; she takes an interest in these things.'

Angus thanked the man and left. His next stop was the library, and the lady in charge proved most helpful on the subject of Northway House and its ghosts.

'You see,' she said, 'Northway House was built from the stones of an old priory that had been laid waste by Thomas Cromwell in the reign of Henry VIII. There are people around here who believe the place is haunted by the last Prior. And if you look at the old world English garden from high up, you'll see that the rockeries are in fact the footstones of an old priory. It has almost the complete footprint of a medieval priory.'

Angus was of course very interested in all of this, he thanked the lady and made his way to Tewksbury Abbey which was situated on a bend in the river. The main doors of the abbey were locked as the abbey was only open for harvest festivals and high days and holidays, but there was a wicket gate in the main doors and Angus stepped into the abbey. And there within this symphony of stone illuminated by a shaft light of a stained glass window was a tomb, on top of which was the effigy of the monk Angus had seen.

Angus relayed all this information to his father who no doubt used it as a conversation piece for many a day afterwards.

Light in the Darkness

By William Armstrong

'You mean…' I said slowly.

'Unfortunately, yes.' Doctor Jackson's voice sounded strange in my new dark world. 'That bang on your head seriously damaged the optic nerves. I'm afraid your blindness is permanent.'

Please God, no! I thought desperately. Writing is my life. Marooned in this black hell I'll go mad. What am I going to do?

'Mother.'

I sensed Yvonne's presence at my shoulder. The faintest hint of her perfume. 'We need to talk.'

'No!' I screamed. 'It's all your fault anyway. If you'd been there when I needed you I wouldn't have had to use those damned steps.'

There was a sharp intake of breath. My daughter's temper was legendary and I was pushing her hard.

'Mother, that's not fair. I'm a housewife, a mother and a part-time secretary. I can only do so much. That's why Frank and I want you to move in with us.'

'I don't want your charity.' I muttered sullenly. 'Just leave me alone.'

Jackson coughed politely.

Always the gentleman, I thought wryly.

'Mrs Allison, I'm leaving now. I suggest you listen to your daughter. Good-bye.' A door closed softly.

'Mum.' There was a steely undertone in Yvonne's voice. 'You can't stay here on your own. There's really no alternative.'

She's right, I thought bitterly; there is no other way. The darkness seemed to press in on me and I fought against it.

'What about Frank?' I muttered. 'How does he feel?'

'It's his idea. He wants you to come.'

'And your job?' I queried.

'Damn the job! We'll manage.'

'I don't want charity,' I said angrily. 'I'll pay my share.'

'Right.' I sensed Yvonne's exasperation. 'Have it your way. Let's see if we can make a go of things. If not for us, then for your grandson's sake. You know he idolises you.'

'Then why hasn't he been to see me?' I demanded.

There was a long silence, then…'I wasn't going to tell you, but….Craig blames himself for your accident.'

'But why?'

'That afternoon you fell off the steps; I'd asked him earlier to go over and check if you needed anything done. His football training overran and he was late. He was shattered when he got there and found you lying unconscious. He still hasn't got over it.'

'I didn't realise.' I tried to come to terms with Yvonne's revelation. 'Look, it was just one of those things. Ask him to come and see me…please.'

'I will.'

I sensed her relief. Another hurdle cleared. 'Now, I'll take you over to our place. You can get settled in then. Alright?'

'I suppose so,' I agreed listlessly.

We got there about mid-afternoon; so Yvonne said anyway. Imprisoned in my frightening dark world, I tried desperately to visualise their home from previous visits.

A trim, detached, four-bedroom bungalow, surrounded by a large well-kept garden. That was my mind picture, though I was beginning to realise that blindness, at least initially, could play strange tricks with one's senses.

'Here we are.' The car slowed and swung to the left, lurching ever so slightly.

This'll be the driveway, I thought, suddenly alert. Maybe I can make something of this blindness after all.

I heard the handbrake being ratcheted on, then the sound of the engine ceased. There was the click of seatbelts being unclipped and the slight pressure across my breast eased. I couldn't resist a feeling of pride that I'd been able to visualise everything so far. Wryly, I wondered if my years of writing had helped.

'Right.' The car door creaked slightly as it was opened. 'I'll take you in first, then come back for your case.' Heels clicked briefly on the paving, then suddenly I could hear the sound of bees, busy among the summer flowers. A soft breeze caressed my cheek.

'Give me your arm, Mum.' The same brisk businesslike voice again. 'Right; feet so…there. Mind your head. Out you come. Good, there we are. Now, hold on to my arm and we'll go along the path to the front door.' We moved off together. The scent from the roses was a bittersweet reminder of my lost sight.

'Mind the two steps now.'

'I can count,' I said sharply. 'I've been here before you know.'

'Yes.' The faintest hint of laughter in her voice. There was a click as the door was opened and the smell of a well-kept house was suddenly in my nostrils.

'Sit here.' I was guided to a chair. 'I'm just going for your case.' Heels tapped purposefully along the path again.

Left alone, I lay back and let my other senses take over. The twin smells of furniture polish and air freshener came to me. Joey, the budgie, chirped excitedly in his cage. There was the muted sound of something being closed. Footsteps came back along the path, the door slammed and I sensed Yvonne in the room.

'Your perfume is very distinctive.'

'It's called Splendor.' Her voice softened. 'Frank loves it. He says it reminds him of our courting days. Now, relax while I put your case in the spare bedroom.'

Relax, I thought bitterly. I'll have plenty of time for that. What'll I do? That's my writing career finished. Goodbye Freddie Fieldmouse and Simon Sealion. Depression engulfed me and I struggled to hold back the tears.

Footsteps ran up the path. Young, eager footsteps. The front door banged noisily and I sensed someone in the room.

'Is that you, Craig?' My maternal instincts welled up in me. 'Haven't you got a hug for your old Gran?'

Suddenly, I sensed him on his knees beside me. Hs strong young arms hugged me as I pictured him again. The athletic body, the engaging smile and the shock of tousled blond hair. Above all, the striking resemblance to Jim, my late husband.

'Oh, Gran, I'm so sorry.' His tears splashed on my hand. 'Please forgive me.'

'There's nothing to forgive. I should have had more sense than climb up those rickety old steps. Now, tell me, what's been happening at school?'

I felt him relax, and slowly, over the next hour, we rebuilt our relationship. Twice I sensed Yvonne's presence, but she wisely decided to stay out of our animated discussion.

When Frank came home that evening, I thanked him for his kindness in inviting me to stay and the atmosphere thawed perceptibly. Later, we discussed the sale of my house, and Yvonne offered to take me to a reputable estate agent, so that a valuation could be arranged.

Gradually the days stretched into weeks, the weeks into months, and I settled into a routine. My hearing became sharper and my sense of smell, which had always been good, was now exceptional. At the same time I got Craig to guide me round the house and the garden, until I had built up a mental picture of my surroundings.

Yet still the bouts of depression persisted. Yvonne and Frank tried to lift my spirits, while Craig was always ready to sit and talk, but nothing compensated for the loss of my literary skills. For years I'd been a prolific writer and now...nothing.

And then, one afternoon, Craig came home from school in a state of suppressed excitement. I picked up good vibes, as the youngsters say, as soon as he entered the room.

'Alright,' I said. 'Let me guess. You've been selected for the under-fourteen district trials.'

'No, Gran. It's something that concerns you.' His voice was alive with enthusiasm. 'Mr Andrews wants you to give a talk on your career. How you began; the books you've written; Simon the Sealion, Rory the Red Deer, the Freddie Fieldmouse series, and so on.' He paused uncertainly, aware of a sudden change in my attitude. 'Please, Gran. The whole school wants to hear you. It'd be cool.'

'Craig,' I said slowly, 'I'd love to, but it's not on. I use slides, flow charts and diagrams to illustrate my talks. That's not possible now.'

The faint hint of Splendor came to me. Yvonne was in the room, sharp and efficient as usual. 'Yes you can do it. I'll handle the slides and the charts. You give the talk.'

'Well,' I said doubtfully; 'if you're sure.'

'Of course I'm sure.' I sensed her impatience. 'I'm a lady of leisure now. We'll make a good team. Get it all on tape. Then you can plan the presentation. A few dummy runs and we'll be in business.'

And so it proved. I'll say this for Yvonne; she knows how to organise.

Came the great day and we made our way to the local academy.

Yvonne eased me out of my seat and I waited, nerves jangling, while she locked the car.

'Right.' I sensed her moving up beside me. 'Hand on my arm; so. Now, step out. This is the quadrangle. I'll tell you when there are any obstacles.' We moved off smoothly, in unison.

'Steps.' I felt Yvonne's body weight shift slightly and braced myself 'Two steps. Now, up…and again. Good.'

Faintly, I heard the buzz of children's voices; many voices. Then someone spoke. 'Good afternoon, Mrs Allison. Welcome to Hatton Academy.' There was a faint and not unpleasant aroma of tobacco.

'Good afternoon,' I replied awkwardly. 'Mr Andrews, I presume?'

'That's right.' He chuckled. 'You sound like Stanley meeting Livingstone. We're all looking forward to your talk.'

'Let's hope you're not disappointed,' I said cautiously.

'Right.' That was Yvonne. 'Let's go.' We moved ahead, slower this time. Her voice came again, softly. 'Hold on. Turning right, now.'

I sensed people. Lots of people. The buzz of excitement died abruptly as we moved forward.

'There.' Yvonne guided me into a seat. I sank into what felt like a large comfortable armchair. 'The board is already set up,' she whispered. 'I'll just take the cover off and Mr Andrews will introduce you. After that it's your show. I'll handle the aids, just as we planned.'

Andrews was an accomplished speaker. He traced my career over the years and I could sense the children's interest quickening. He's done his homework I thought grudgingly.

'…and, as you know, Mrs Allison lost her sight some time ago. As I'm sure you'll agree, that must be a horrendous thing to happen to a writer. However, she has, very bravely, agreed to talk to us about her career, and I feel we'll all learn a great deal this afternoon. So, let's hear your appreciation for a very talented lady…Mrs Allison.'

The applause, punctuated by cheers and whistles, was deafening.

I rose slowly to my feet, sensing Yvonne's presence.

'Straight ahead,' she whispered. 'I'll put your hand on the mike. Then it's all yours. I'm on your right…at the board.'

'Hi,' I said, gripping the mike stand tightly. 'Thanks for the appreciation. Now I've got to earn it,' and suddenly I knew it was going to be alright. Smoothly, I outlined my early steps in a writing career and my decision to specialise in children's books. From then on I felt the audience warming to me. I'd always had a superb memory and today was proving it.

'And so,' I concluded, 'You now know what it feels like to be a writer. The highs, the lows, the cheers and the tears…but I still wouldn't have missed it for the world. Thank you.'

The applause was deafening, and went on and on until I held up my hand for silence. 'Craig tells me you're cool. Now I believe him!'

This time there was laughter mixed with the applause. I felt Yvonne's hand on my sleeve. 'Mum, you were brilliant.'

'Thanks,' I said shakily. 'Only with your help.'

'Mrs Allison.' I picked up Andrews on my left. 'That was terrific. Would you consider giving a series of lectures?'

'I'll think about it,' I said carefully, 'but right now I'm going home to call my agent. If Yvonne's shorthand is on a par with all her other skills, and she's agreeable, I'm going back to writing!'

McKinnon's Last Fling

By William Clinkenbeard

Alexander McKinnon unlaced the flap of the tipi, folded it back and stepped out into the sunshine. The light dazzled him for a moment. It must be later than he had thought; yet inside the tipi it had been pitch-black. Even standing in the sunshine he could see his breath, for it was September, the Moon of the Young Calves Growing Black. The smoke from a hundred fires curled up and above the cluster of lodges and dispersed into the blue. By now he should be familiar with the image of white clouds floating in a brilliant blue sky, but he wasn't. All those Scottish moons he had lived under at home had instilled gray skies, and gloom within his soul.

McKinnon had just finished leading a party of Europeans and Easterners on a six weeks' tour of the prairies. All together there had been thirty sportsmen accompanied by twenty gentlemen, muleteers and servants. The party even included a German artist, Alfred Bromschwig. They had watched the great buffalo herds thundering across the plains, shaking the earth beneath them. They had studied the buffalo watering in the wide Platte at night, strangely quiet and domestic in the moonlight. They had hunted the buffalo as well, but always under McKinnon's strict control. The hunters could shoot only as many beasts as could be profitably used. He had to keep the good will of his friends, who received most of the kill. Further Northwest they had hunted elk, pronghorn antelope and even bear on the eastern slope of the Rockies. They shot ducks on Wood Lake in the sandhills and gazed upwards to follow the flights of the sandhill cranes. While the sportsmen indulged their passion for shooting, the gentlemen studied the land, dreaming dreams of exploitation. All along the way, Bromschwig had made sketches of the plains, but it wasn't easy. How could you gain perspective on a flat tabletop deep in buffalo grass as high as a man's chest without a valley or rise in sight? There was nowhere to get any elevation. But the great herds could be drawn standing in the inch-deep and mile-wide Platte. The party of travellers, a winding snake of horses, mules and riders could be drawn sidling across the prairie. And there were some geological features that gave depth: the bluffs along the North Platte and the tall chimney-like rock that signalled the route to the Wild West. The plan was for Bromschwig to enlarge and paint several of these sketches to hang on the walls of McKinnon's castle. This would constitute his payment for the trip. McKinnon had already decided where to hang them.

McKinnon had first visited Nebraska Territory back in 1833, making his way slowly up the Platte. Already it was becoming the main highway to the West. He met French trappers with their pelts resting under cottonwood trees at bends in the river, mountain men returning from the high country bearing tall tales, and youthful soldiers arriving at Fort Kearny. Over the course of several years he had explored most of the territory and made friends with the Lakota. Then he started on the long trip home, but he had been careful to publicise himself along the way. On the eastern seaboard he told his stories about the West and elicited promises from the well-to-do who yearned for adventure. The same stories were later told on the other side of the Atlantic, in London and Edinburgh. Before long he had signed up enough eager adventurers to make an expedition in the following year feasible.

McKinnon had been helped by the fact that he was an appealing character. His dark hair curling up from under a large black hat, his hooked nose over a well-trimmed moustache, combined with intense blue eyes made an immediate and striking impression. In spite of being outdoors so much of his time he was pale. His looks and bearing, combined with a pronounced Scottish accent made him a favoured dinner guest in the homes of the wealthy in New York and New Jersey. He regaled the other diners with tales of the Wild West.

The tour was now over, and he had shepherded the party as far back as Nebraska City, where they caught the paddle steamer *Jennie Brown* down the Big Muddy bound for St. Louis and the outer world. He had stayed two days in the town, booming through the trade on the Missouri River. He bought knives, tobacco, molasses, brown sugar, coffee and a few blankets. He would head back to the camp to spend some time with his friends the Oglala and Brule, both tribes of the Lakota or Sioux Nation.

McKinnon would himself soon be travelling back to Scotland. Yet the idea of returning home had begun to generate feelings of regret and resignation. The contrast between Cannich and this prairie weighed heavily on the mind. He could never decide about where he really belonged. Should he be at home acting as husband and father, having porridge in the dining hall of the castle, and fulfilling his role as the laird of a highland estate, or here acting as adventurer, breakfasting on dried buffalo and smoking the pipe with Man Afraid and Conquering Bear? The question kept coming up and he kept brushing it aside.

Man Afraid suddenly stood before him, making the traditional Sioux greeting, 'Hou'. McKinnon greeted him and rubbed his eyes with his knuckles to convey his sleepiness. Conversing with the Lakota was always frustrating, but he had learned some key Lakota words and phrases, and his friends had picked up a few English words. Man Afraid could never quite get his tongue around 'McKinnon', so it always came out 'Takinnon'. Man Afraid was his best friend in the camp. Over six feet tall and muscular, he was regarded as an expert horseman and a good warrior. Yet it had taken McKinnon some time to square the man with his name. Eventually it became clear. He was really 'Man Whose Enemies are Afraid of his Horse'. But this had proved too cumbersome even for the Lakota. So it gradually became 'Man Afraid of his Horse', and finally for conversational ease, 'Man Afraid'. Everyone knew that the shortened version was in no way an accurate description of the person himself.

'Takinnon?' said Man Afraid, inflecting a question, and putting his hands together under a tilted head.

'Yes,' said Mckinnon, 'I slept well'.

'You talk chief Bear?' Man Afraid, said, pointing in the direction of the great chief's tipi.

McKinnon nodded. Yesterday he had had to search for some time to find the camp, even though there were many lodges. The Brule and Oglala often made camp together. So he had arrived late in the evening and had not seen Conquering Bear. The chief was actually a Brule, the people of the 'burnt thighs'. It would not have been fitting for the chief to emerge from his lodge at that time to welcome even a close friend. But today, when the chief was ready, they would talk.

'We talk, ride, smoke later,' said Man Afraid.

McKinnon nodded as his friend turned to walk away. Man Afraid would organise his reunion with the chief.

McKinnon stretched and turned around to get his bearings in the circle of tipis. Some Lakota children stood in a cluster partially behind his lodge, watching him quietly but without fear. He smiled but received no return smiles, only a steady gaze from their black eyes. Most of them were too small to remember him from over a year ago. The community was occupied with the customary domestic chores. Squaws gossiped while they scraped hides and pegged them out to dry, children shouted as they played their games, dogs barked and horses stamped their hooves and snorted. He had been exhausted last night, and it had been good to slide under the heavy buffalo robe and drop off to sleep. This was something that Marion could not understand. It gave her the furies when Alexander slid silently out of their bed and onto the floor of the bedroom to sleep under the buffalo robe.

'Why do you have to be a savage here?' she would always ask. 'Isn't it enough to be a savage when you're in America?'

He couldn't answer. He just felt more comfortable under a buffalo robe on the floor. It brought back good memories and suited his way of being in the world. It seemed to be some kind of symbolic protest as well, a way of expressing his dissatisfaction with the comfort and routine of his life in Cannich.

Marion dismissed his adventures and feelings all too lightly. He had tried on many occasions to explain to her and their daughters the sense of freedom and exhilaration that came to him on the prairie, but to no avail. They listened with interest to his stories, but that did not finally mitigate their unhappiness about his absences. Perhaps had they had a son it might have been different. Marion's resentment seemed to smoulder like a peat fire. Someone, she said, had to stay and run the estate while he was away being a great adventurer, and that someone was her. Still, this trip would bring in enough money to help sustain their estate at Cannich for several years, and she could hardly complain.

McKinnon readied himself for his meeting with the chief. He had, unlike other white men, been able to travel through the Lakota Territory unmolested. Now it was time to express his thanks. His gifts would be presented to Conquering Bear after they had smoked for a while. During his last visit, the chief had wanted to hear about McKinnon's country. As chief, he had been called on to talk to white men more often than others, so he had more white men's words. McKinnon had tried to describe the hills covered by the ancient Caledonian Forest, the long deep loch and the fast-flowing rivers. The chief liked to hear about the salmon returning up the river every year, leaping over the obstacles to spawn. There were no salmon in the Platte, and only small fish in the other rivers that Conquering Bear knew. None of them jumped out of the water. Their standing joke was the size of the fish. Each time they talked the fish grew larger. But Bear's face always became serious when they spoke about the absence of buffalo in McKinnon's country. He could not imagine a place without buffalo. Men might eat the big fish, but how could they make tipis or robes or tools without buffalo? In the dust of the tipi floor McKinnon had drawn pictures of the castle nestling in the hills with the river running by. On the top of the castle he added a man playing pipes that stuck out of a bag. Conquering Bear found it hard to imagine.

Now wandering around the camp, nodding to people as he went, McKinnon found it even more painful to think about going back. Of course it was home and of course he wanted to see Marion and the girls. But it was always grey and chilly and damp. A man could see no farther than the next dark hill, and the land was cut into pieces by stone walls. Life seemed permanently fixed in a routine established by weather, culture and Kirk. They had friends and relatives, but their conversations and social gatherings bored him. Here on the prairie a man could be free to ride wherever he wished, free to hunt, free to share stories of real exploits. The sun was warm on his face and back, and even in the bitterly cold weather the land sparkled. When the people danced here it was for a reason: to prepare for a hunt or to celebrate some event or to mark the changing seasons. But these insights were hard to describe. No one at home really wanted to know. Another prolonged absence from home would not be acceptable to Marion. He sighed in the acknowledgement that this would have to be the last trip.

Man Afraid appeared again and signalled for McKinnon to enter Conquering Bear's lodge. The chief greeted him warmly and they smoked a pipe while McKinnon related his tales about his band of tourists. He told about their difficulties in staying in the saddle while chasing the buffalo, about the seasickness the endless prairie induced within them, and about how Alfred kept losing his way after staying behind to make his sketches. He had to be rescued so often! There was much laughter. The great chief told of his fears about the growing tide of travellers along the trail. More and more people were coming along the Platte. The grass trail, flattened by wagons and animals, was growing wider and wider, and there were now ruts from wagon wheels on the prairie. He told McKinnon about the single Mormon man coming along the trail with his cow. Frightened by some young Brule riders, the cow rampaged through the camp, catching a baby in its cradleboard on its horns. Having been dragged and thrown, the baby had died. The Lakota had captured the cow, butchering and eating it the same day. While it was a tough old thing, it seemed like a reasonable exchange to the Lakota, but the man was now making trouble for them at Fort Kearny. Among all the Lakotas and their neighbours there was growing resentment about this uninvited white invasion.

The afternoon was soon spent. McKinnon unpacked his gifts and spread them outside the tipi, surrounded by a circle of curious women and children. He was invited to eat with the chief, and the guest horn spoon was brought to dip into the kettle. At the end of the meal, Conquering Bear suggested that his friend should have a woman for comfort. The nights were growing chilly and he had been away a long time; he ought to have a companion. The offer was not an easy thing for McKinnon to refuse, coming as it did from a great chief. Besides, in all honesty, he would welcome the company of the woman. No one at home need ever know, and it would only be for a few weeks.

McKinnon spent the next two weeks simply being there, sharing tales with the Lakota, smoking and hunting with Man Afraid, and making new friends around the fire. At night he and the woman lay together under the buffalo robes. They spoke little, but she was warm, and she cooked and cared for him. It was good. He kept trying to prepare himself to return home, to think himself back into his own place and feel good about it, but it was hard.

Just before the Moon of the Falling Leaves, McKinnon said farewell to the Oglala and Brule, left the camp and made his way down the trail. Sumac had turned the breaks along the river red, and above them the cottonwoods shimmered in yellow and gold. Here and there bittersweet dangled, trembling threads of orange in the sun. The snows would come soon, and he could not afford to be snowbound in the long winter. There were few travelers on the trail now, and overhead the skies were filled with ducks and geese on their journey south.

By leaving the Lakota camp forever, there were many things that McKinnon would never know. He would never know that even during the time it took to make his way down the Missouri, then up the Mississippi, then across the North Atlantic and back to Cannich, the woman would take a husband in the customary Lakota fashion. He would never know that after some months she would give birth to a baby. The boy, initially called Curly, would always appear slightly different than his brothers. He was paler, quieter, and more reflective. As a young warrior he would always be standing slightly apart from them, without much liking for the noise of the drumming, chanting, and dancing. He was sufficiently different to be spoken of as *Our Strange Man*. Yet always he was held in great respect, and when he walked through the camp every person turned to look, to acknowledge his presence, and to speak. His mother's husband was an Oglala holy man.

It was said of Curly that he could dream himself into a different world, the real world that lay behind this one. This world had trees and grass and sky as well, but existed in a sacred way. In his dreams Curly often had a powerful vision of himself on horseback, the horse's neck lifted high and its feet flying free, carrying him fearlessly towards his enemies, impervious to their arrows or lead balls. His vision of himself would be recorded by Bad Heart Bull, the Oglala historian who believed that a people without history were like the wind on the buffalo grass. On Bad Heart Bull's skin paintings, Curly would always be drawn close to the holy man and to McKinnon. Later, Curly came to be called Crazy Horse. All these things McKinnon would never know.

Yet there was one thing that McKinnon would know. For years after his return, he made it a habit to look for news of the West in the newspaper he got from Inverness from time to time. On chilly autumn evenings he would sit before a roaring fire beneath Alfred Bromschwig's large oil of the buffalo herd watering in the river, scouring the paper for news. On one particular day he found yet another report about the Indian wars in the American West. From it he would learn that the Seventh Cavalry under Colonel George Custer had suffered a catastrophic defeat at the hands of the Sioux and Cheyenne at the Battle of the Little Big Horn. According to the article, one warrior in particular had been responsible for the strategy of this victory over the blustering, over-ambitious Long Hair. This was a warrior who having dreamed himself into the sacred world, could charge the soldiers directly with rifle held high, then disappear to shoot from under the neck of his horse, and then ride away to decoy them into a trap. This warrior, according to the newspaper, bore the name Crazy Horse.

His Majesties Service

By Allan Moore

I joined the Royal Navy on October 1950. Along with many other men, we were given a rail warrant at the recruiting office in Albert Square at Manchester to travel to Southsea near Portsmouth in Hampshire. We journeyed to Southsea via Waterloo station in London to Portsmouth, and there we were directed by the rail transport officer (RTO) to board lorries, which took us to Victoria Barracks in Southsea.

The first week in Victoria Barracks was spent in acclimatisation. This consisted of marching around, still in our civilian clothes, to lectures from the Commanding Officer, the Padre, and the Medical Officer, amongst others. We saw documentary films about damage control, fire fighting and graphic scenes of people suffering from the many types of Venereal Disease; had this been our first sight of the undraped female, it would have been one of extreme prejudice. We were treated to the howls of men being tortured by an instrument called the umbrella, which was inserted into the infected part of the body then opened and revolved. The cure for gonorrhoea using anti-biotic was painless and effective. I never met any sailors in the next decade who had been subjected to the 'umbrella'. So, perhaps it was just scare tactics.

At the end of the week having been treated reasonably politely, we were marched off to the Pay Office where our squad was brought to attention and informed that this was our last chance to get out of the "RN".

'Just take one step forward and fall out. You will be given a rail warrant to get you home,' said the Petty Officer. 'Once you accept the first pay there's no way out, its called taking the King's shilling.' There were many times in the next decade that I wished that I had taken that one step forward, especially when I came out of the Pay Office with ten shillings to last me for the next two weeks.

All semblance of politeness was gone. An officer hectored us: he had one thin gold ring on his sleeve; this denoted a warrant officer, a man who had come up from the ranks. Any illusion that we were to be commanded by officers and gentlemen was harshly dispelled. No one had ever shouted four letter words at me in the previous sixteen years of my life; the prospect of this being my lot for the next twenty-two years was daunting.

Later that day we were kitted up with hairy blue serge uniforms, nos. 1s, 2s and 8s, the latter being blue denim working dress. Much of the kit supplied was useless, since I had grown out of it when the time came to use it. The white tropical and red sea kit had to be maintained clean and smart for kit musters.

It soon became obvious to me that no one expected you to really wear the 'Pussers Issue.' The wearing of it marked you out as raw recruits. I carted the 'Pussers Issue' around for many years and finally handed it in as one was required to do when I left the service.

Although we were not allowed shore leave for some weeks, a number of naval tailors came in to the barracks, so I was measured up for a decently cut suit, the 'tailors rep.' They also supplied me immediately with an off the peg suit. I hoped that my father would come up with the money before it was due, as there was no way the tailor would extend credit to a boy earning ten shillings a fortnight.

After some weeks of 'square bashing', we had a passing out parade and were granted leave to go ashore. This entailed marching out through the barrack gates and dispersing. The trip ashore was something of an anti—climax. We were so obviously rookies, not even the ladies of the oldest profession wished to know us. My pay of ten shillings a fortnight wouldn't have bought a kind word.

Early next morning early, we boarded lorries and were driven all day to our next training base in Yorkshire. We arrived at the gates of HMS Ceres on a cold winter night. Link fencing topped with barbed wire was stretched out into the darkness beyond the harsh lighting at the gates. We crowded into the Guard Room and were asked our service numbers, checked off against a list and issued with a station-card, which had my name, service number and rank already printed on it. It further informed me that I was in the second starboard watch. We mustered outside the Guardhouse, collected our hammocks, our kitbags and cases and then trudged after a seaman to our accommodation block. We were given three minutes to wash, change our clothes and muster outside. The last man to fall in was awarded a kit muster. We marched to the dinning hall and sat in a corner of this vast empty place. We waited hopefully and silently to faint sounds of crockery and cutlery. Then suddenly there was a rattle and a crash as the serving hatch opened. The stew was free of cockroaches unlike the stuff served at Victoria Barracks. We pleaded for the implements to eat it with, but the cook said too f—g bad, so we had to use bread to scoop it up. A Petty Officer came in and stood watching us eat, he remarked that we would be given eating irons and an enamel mug tomorrow. 'Meantime hear this, I am Petty Officer Williams. You don't normally call PO's sir, but for the duration of your training, you do so address me! For the next few months I will be your mother and father, if you let me down,—-well just don't. Got it?' We all chorused, 'Yes sir' and were marched back to the accommodation hut. Petty Officer Williams told us that wakey wakey was at five AM sharp.

'Muster in gym kit; last man out gets a kit-muster; sleep in your own beds, I have an aversion to poofters!'

The day started early and everything was done at the double, you ran to the dinning hall and you ran from it. If you were sick, you ran to the sick-bay; whilst waiting to see the doctor you were set to scrubbing and polishing; the only person who allowed a modicum of relaxation was the padre, he allowed you to stand at ease.

There were three boys in our intake, I was the youngest but looked older than the others; one boy was chosen by the Captain to be his personal servant. He told me years later that his duties extended to bed warming. The other boy committed suicide; he could not cope with the sexual harassment.

I found it difficult to decide whether to treat the behaviour of the older men as a joke or report it as an offence. The boy who killed himself worried that he was to blame that men came on to him; he had golden hair and his voice was unbroken.

Shortly after our arrival at HMS Ceres, I was required to take part in the ceremony whereby the captain and the youngest rating take hold of an oar and mix the Christmas pudding. They had wanted the youngest looking boy but tradition demanded it be the youngest by birth date.

Our instructor PO Williams was on our case every day. He taught us to march line abreast, to right and left incline, to present arms, shoulder arms, etc. One bad day when it was too icy to perform with fixed bayonets on the parade ground; PO Williams had us in a classroom holding forth about watertight doors and Thetis Clipps and their use. He suddenly asked me why the ship we were aboard was called HMS Ceres.

I said,'Well, I suppose that being a supply and secretariat training establishment dealing with food it was to do with cereals, The Goddess of Agriculture.'

PO Williams said 'Clever bugger aint ee! And oo' named this stone frigate that boyoh? Probably some civil servant at the Admiralty.'

'And why's that?'

'Because I never came across a naval officer who'd had a classical education.'

Shortly after this exchange the captain sent his midshipman over to me to tell me to go to the captain. I marched across and stood stiffly at attention; he asked me a few questions then said, 'I suggested the name of this ship to their lordships.'

Then he grinned and said, 'Tread carefully Moore, my spies are everywhere.'

Many years later, the captain, now an Admiral, was dinning with a captain of supply who was going on somewhat about palatable and gastronomically matching food and wine. The captain's wife declared that her husband was a real gourmand. I stifled a laugh, but the Admiral looked up and said to the captain, 'I think naval officers should have a classical education.'

He then grinned across at me.

After a few more months, our initial training ended and we all went off on Christmas leave.

Woman in Purple
(A Cautionary Tale for People of a Certain Age)

By Rosemary Damianos

Fifty is a dangerous age, but it didn't seem so at the time.

Looking back, I think I first began to have an inkling the morning I changed a habit of a lifetime and went shopping on a Wednesday instead of on my usual day. I'm sure that's when it began.

I was pushing my overloaded trolley, mentally preparing meals, when I almost collided with a kneeling figure dismantling a display of colourful folders. The discarded cardboard sign at her feet said 'Back to School' in primary colours, and I saw to my dismay that she had a stack of Christmas cards beside her. The trolley skewed to the side as I hastily came to an abrupt halt, and I had to apologize to the startled woman.

Fortunately, it also jogged my brain into a higher gear and an inner voice, sounding exactly like my late mother, informed me crisply that at least three quarters of my shopping was *quite unnecessary*. I muttered a curse under my breath and wheeled the trolley back towards the cereal aisle and began to unload it. Fellow shoppers and some staff watched my erratic progress as I mentally unticked my shopping list and returned the contents of my trolley to the correct shelves. I should, of course, have just abandoned it and marched out of the store. I would have done, but it was my local store and the manager was looking at me.

I took full advantage of their generous discounts in the wine department and rummaged in my bag for my car keys while the girl went to fetch a couple of those carrier cases for the bottles. That was when my mother spoke to me again; and reminded me tersely that my youngest child had driven off with it, when he returned to university with half of my worldly goods and most of the contents of the larder.

It was unfortunate that my sotto voce curse was intercepted by the vicar and his wife, standing at the next check out and eyeing my purchases with disapproval. It was an uncomfortable journey home, squeezed in the back of their car with my shopping and their unspoken thoughts; and I did not invite them in for coffee.

The postman had been and I picked up the mail, putting all the bills in my husband's pile and opened up the letter from my doctor. She congratulated me, far too heartily to my way of thinking, on my recent birthday and invited me to attend her next clinic for mature women. My face became even redder as I thought about the morning's calamities and wondered if this was an instance of what my children had started referring to as *senior moments*.

The letterbox rattled again and I went to see what had just been delivered. I lost the plot entirely then as I picked up the Saga brochure that sat on my polished floor, and I shouted at the top of my voice that I knew I was fifty but I was not old. My husband popped his head round the door of the sitting room and asked me anxiously if I wanted a nice cup of tea. I had a nice gin and tonic instead, before putting away the shopping.

A few days later, I was handed a sheaf of glossy brochures from a Japanese car company and my husband, who is three years younger than me and yet to cross the barrier that separates Saga and non-Saga people, beamed as he told me that he was going to buy me a brand new car to celebrate my birthday and the emptying of our nest. He took charge of the brochures and almost started drooling as he read them aloud.

I have never understood why gadgets so entranced the males in my household and to be honest, I just let them get on with it. I left my husband to place the order and what with one thing and another, it slipped my mind.

Many things have started slipping my mind lately and I have had to write myself notes. The other ladies at the clinic were very reassuring and it was something of a relief to discover that I was not the only daughter to be in communication with a deceased parent. Seeing my mother's face in the mirror when I brushed my teeth in the morning was not nearly as strange as hearing her in my head or sounding like her when I ranted at my children.

I had just reached the library when my phone rang. I didn't answer it and turned it off before going in to join the others in the book group. We were working our way through Virginia Woolf's novels and had been given *To the*

Lighthouse to read. That, I think, was the last straw. I thought long and hard about Mrs. Dalloway on my way home and my discontentment grew.

I picked up the Saga brochure and then poured myself out a large glass of Merlot. I flicked through the pages and then looked at the price list. It was so tempting; but unlike an adventurous aunt, I had never kept a 'bolting jar' and I just couldn't lay my hands on sufficient funds. My children had had their gap year and I felt strong pangs of envy at the ease with which they just took off, sloughing off their juvenile skins and returning in their adult state. I held the brochure and wished the thing could be done in reverse. Well, why not?

My mother listed all the reasons why not, even though I tried very hard not to listen to her, and I turned off the television. Somehow, I had missed the boat and probably so had most of my generation. We were the lost souls caught firmly between the dutiful and the liberated, despised by both probably.

I got up and stared defiantly at the mirror and stuck out my tongue in juvenile defiance before noticing the envelope on the mantelpiece. The cheque for the car was inside and I gulped when I saw just how much the car cost. I read the short note from my husband, apologizing for his enforced absence and asking me to pay the cheque into my account, so that I could pay for the car.

I had every intention of buying the car, but the day before I was due to pick it up, a leaflet fell out of the Radio Times and I went to the travel agency in town instead.

I'm sorry, I've been chatting on and on and haven't introduced myself yet. My name is Margaret Gray and my husband is called Iain. My children would rather remain anonymous, but I have three grown up sons. I am not at home at the moment, in fact I am a missing person, but I am confident that I will find myself one day.

At the moment I am standing out on the deck of a cruise ship looking at whales. We are somewhere in the Antarctic and we have come on a nature cruise. I am known as Virginia Dalloway to my fellow passengers and I have to keep remembering that. It is not as easy as it seems and you have to keep your wits about you. My fellow passengers are all American; and apart from the guide/lecturer, are all older than me. Now there's a strange thing; they don't have the same slippers and cocoa outlook. If anything, they pursue youth mercilessly and refuse to acknowledge aging until it's forced upon them.

I've discovered muscles that I didn't know I possessed since I found myself in the ship's gym; and I see that I have a great deal of leeway to make up.

We will be returning to San Francisco in a few days and then I think I will travel up to Canada. I have been away from home for a month, although it doesn't seem that long and I did send my husband an e-mail before I flew to San Francisco.

That probably astonished him; I think I'll try one of those Internet café places when I arrive. I did feel rather guilty about cashing the cheque and taking a year's housekeeping from our joint account, but I had to buy clothes and a suitcase too. That's the problem with spur of the moment decisions, you see. It's only in films and soap operas that the mundane practicalities of life are ignored. I'm sorry, I'm chattering on again.

Do I regret bolting?

That's not an easy question to answer. At first I was caught up in the excitement of it. There I was, standing outside the travel agency gazing at a picture of Bill Bryson. I'm on the cruise he'll lead in a few weeks time, although I didn't know that at the time. I wanted a warmer destination, but this cruise was available and I got a discount when I told them I'd pay cash. I even managed to upgrade my ticket on the flight out and I decided to do the same on the ship. It's not grand or luxurious; but it is comfortable, and the food is good. My cabin is roomy and I can look out at the sea when I want to. My fellow passengers are a group from a whale and dolphin conservation society and most of them are retired academics.

I do not quite fit in, but they have taken pity on me and include me in their social activities. My bridge playing is not quite up to their standards either, but they seem happy to accept that it's probably due to the difference between American and English conventions. My usual partner is not only erudite but also a keen reader and I've had a few tense moments. I really do think I should have been less fanciful in choosing my *nom de sejour*. But it's too late now.

By the time I left the travel agency with my tickets, it had started raining heavily; and I dived into the nearest shop. It hit me, after I'd ordered a ruinously expensive coffee, that I had done a very foolish thing. I could not return the tickets. I would have to go through with it. And what's more, would be leaving in forty-eight hours for an Antarctic cruise. That was when I knew I was having a very senior moment and I started to giggle and thought of my namesake and her 'bolting jar'.

Great Aunt Meg had never managed to bolt; but she told me once that the possibility of being able to do so, kept her sane. She would have made a wonderful wife and mother, but the dearth of young men after the carnage of the Great War left her a spinster. She was the eldest of six sisters and the youngest one, my mother, was the only one of them to get married. Aunt Meg kept house for my grandfather after grandmother died, and saw all her sisters leave. I think that's why she cherished her 'bolting jar'. I wonder what happened to it?

I raised my mug to her memory and then walked through the Plaza to John Lewis. I drew a blank and tried Debenham's next. It was sheer bliss! I'd never used their personal shopping service before and it was a real eye-opener! I left the store with everything I needed and several things I didn't, but the shopping fever had me firmly in its grip.

My hands shook as I sat in front of the computer and I sat staring at it for ages before trying to explain my absence. I honestly can't remember which version I finally sent, it must have been about the eighth or ninth. The subject was the hardest part and I tried all kinds of phrases until I just wrote, 'Sorry about the car'.

I knew that would grab his attention and that his relief that I hadn't written it off would make my absence not seem quite so bad. This of course is just a theory, I will find out when I contact him. Of course, he will probably still be in a bad mood because I wasn't there to collect him from the airport.

It felt very odd to be travelling alone, I've never travelled alone before and I kept thinking that I'd forgotten something and kept looking around for my husband and children. I was shown into the first class lounge, I had booked business class but I was upgraded again, and found myself almost alone. For a moment I thought of fleeing back into the noisy chaos of the departure lounge, but the charming young steward led me over to a comfortable sofa and asked me what I'd like to drink. It's difficult really to explain how I felt. Euphoria; probably the gin: a feeling of lightness and freedom and butterflies.

I wish I could describe the flight, but I slept through most of it. It seems such a waste, paying all that money and then sleeping, but I can always pay more attention on the way home.

We had a couple of days in San Francisco before the cruise and I tried to see everything! In my youth, I wanted to go to San Francisco and wear flowers in my hair but I was forced to keep my mind on my studies. We didn't have gap years then either, not in my family, and I went up to university straight from school. I read English and Philosophy and got married two years after I graduated and then the children appeared. I never wanted my life to turn out like that and I envied my friends their freedom. They probably envied me too, but I never had the chance to ask them and apart from my very best friend, they gradually dropped out of sight. It came as something of a shock when our eldest son went to my old college as a student, and I ran into the wildest member of my old gang. She had gone to America and had picked up a rather exotic looking guy at a music festival and had dropped out for some years. When we met again on Freshers Day, I discovered that she had become a noted academic and was now dressed in sensible clothes and my jaw dropped.

I said goodbye to my fellow travellers and watched them disembark. I felt sad and almost wished I hadn't come, but I knew that I would have to finish my adventure.

I'd become so used to responding to Virginia Dalloway, I paid no heed to the paged announcement for Margaret Gray; and I walked out into the street. It was very busy and I didn't hear the footsteps behind me. I felt someone grab me and I clutched my handbag to me, feeling sick with fear. My attacker spun me round and I kicked out and saw him crumple up and drop to the pavement. I heard him groan and call out my name and saw my husband lying on the dirty pavement. Everything seemed to happen in slow motion as I bent to comfort him and fend off the crowd. The policeman called for an ambulance and we went to the local emergency room. He sat with me and tried to get my story straight and looked at me as if I were just another crazy woman. I showed him my tickets and passport and eventually he stood up and wished me a nice day, before leaving.

We talked non stop on our journey to Canada; and started looking for ourselves again. It was painful at times as I saw his hurt and bewilderment, but that's the difference between Saga and non-Saga people I suppose. Once you've crossed over that great divide, life is never the same again if you're lucky.

Jock's Plan

By Maureen Brister

The sun was coming up as Jock Steedman wearily pushed open the gate to his home. Jock was a miner on constant night shift in the local pit and all he asked every morning was a few hours of peace and quiet to catch up on some much needed sleep. But he had had to settle for something less recently and he was getting a bit fed up with it. His six (yes, six) daughters ranged in age from 17 to 26. Jock had desperately wanted a son, but when his wife Jean found herself pregnant with twins and they too were girls, they decided enough was enough and Jock settled for 'his girls'. Now that they were all working and enjoying the local dance halls in the evening life was even more dizzy than usual.

The war showed no sign of coming to an end. There were servicemen stationed nearby from Canada and the USA as well as other parts of the United Kingdom and his girls had no shortage of dance partners and so far, short term boyfriends!

Jock and Jean knew what their neighbours thought of the lively girls and their constantly changing uniformed male companions but they trusted their daughters and knew they were all having the time of their lives, war or no war. The girls worked hard during the day and were always happy to help out their many aunts and uncles with shopping etc. so their parents did not begrudge them their evening enjoyment.

There was however one complaint. Jock had and that lay in the area of where he would be sleeping. The girls and their mother regularly put up boyfriends who missed their late night transport back to base and to accommodate these young men Jean and the girls shifted the furniture on what seemed to Jock almost a nightly basis just now. The result was that every time Jock put his key in the lock he never knew who he was likely to find or where. He had even tripped over bodies in the lobby before now.

Normally these 'bodies' were up and out of the way fairly soon after Jock arrived home as they had to be sure of being back on base before their absence was noticed and that meant catching the first buses in the morning. Fine by Jock. But for the past couple of weeks there had been an exception to this. Meg, his middle and feistiest daughter, had a more long-term relationship on the go. Well, long-term compared to the usual week or two Jock supposed. Anyway Meg was able to twist her mother round her little finger, and it seemed that this particular boyfriend who went by the name of Tommy, had a bad back so he had to have a particular bed and mattress and that just happened to be in the quietest bedroom at the back of the house where the noise from the street traffic was at its lowest and where Jock could always be sure of having an uninterrupted few hours sleep every day. Worse than that was that Tommy did not have to be up early in the mornings to rush back to base, he did not go on duty till lunchtime so Jock had to wait till his wife and the girls were up and about to see where he could grab a bed and of course it was never as comfortable nor as quiet as the bed in the back bedroom! The one thing Jock had noticed though was that Tommy always left things to the last minute and slept as long as he thought he could get away with before dashing downstairs, out the front door, through the gate and on to the 11 o'clock local bus.

Jock was sick of it. He had a plan. He thoughtfully stirred the pot of porridge and chewed over his idea. It would mean he wouldn't get to bed as early as usual this morning, but that in turn could mean his favourite bed would be free. All this was going through his mind as he poured out his porridge and added just the right amount of milk and salt to bring it to the right taste. He loved his porridge and the pot was always big enough to feed whoever happened to be up and about at that time of the morning, usually Jean. The girls didn't often have time for breakfast these days.

After a wash and tidy up he took himself out to walk to the nearby farm where his two brothers worked. They agreed it was a great plan and chuckled at the thought of it. Jock went home to bed and despite the fact that Tommy was still in the back bedroom and he had to sleep in the front of the house he got a good few hours in and then went to work in his fruit and vegetable garden. Jean and the girls spent weeks making jams and jellies from the strawberries, raspberries and blackcurrants in the garden and the vegetables that were not eaten were stored and saw them through most of the winter. Jock enjoyed the work associated with gardening. After being down the mine it made a change to be outdoors and getting the fresh air plus it got him out of Jean's way in the afternoons while she was busy cooking tea for the family. There was very rarely a free burner on their oven summer or winter. Jean was a plain cook but a good cook and the family were well fed compared to others.

The house was chaotic as usual after teatime that day as the girls once again got themselves ready for the dancing. This involved a lot of borrowing of clothes, doing of hair and generally a lot of laughter. Jock casually asked Meg if she would be meeting Tommy that night and was glad to hear that she would. She thought he was more than just one of her normal boyfriends Jock was told, and he could be around for a while. She hoped her father didn't mind. Jock shrugged his shoulders and puffed away on his pipe, trying to appear as nonchalant about this news as he could.

Next morning when Jock came home there did not seem to be as many 'lodgers' as normal but he checked that the door to the upstairs back bedroom was firmly closed and it was. Tommy was once again in residence.

Breakfast was over and the house had emptied of the girls and their boyfriends, except Tommy, when Jock heard a loud whistle from outside. He opened the front door to see his brothers sitting on a horse drawn cart and signalled to them that it was OK to divest themselves of their steaming load and showed them exactly where to put it. Jean appeared at his side and when she saw what was going on, she shook her head and laughed and laughed. She knew exactly what was about to happen and was determined to see it all!

At about quarter to eleven Jock and Jean heard the upstairs bedroom door open, the sound of the toilet flushing and water running. They took up their positions by the front window. Tommy came rushing down the stairs, still half asleep, opened the front door, and jumped down the steps right into the load of fresh manure that Jock's brothers had delivered just an hour earlier! The passengers on the 11 o'clock bus had a grandstand view of the whole thing as did Jock and Jean. Jock would not let Jean go to the door to see if Tommy wanted to have a wash and tidy up, as far as he was concerned his plan had worked. Tommy would definitely not be on the scene in the immediate future. Meg may not speak to him for a few days but she would get over it and more to the point, Jock could get back to his favourite bed in the quietest room in the house and maybe, just maybe, Jean would put her foot down and not give his bed away so readily in the future. Jock put on his gardening boots, got out his wheelbarrow and started to move the manure to the vegetable plot, smiling quietly to himself. Today he would change his routine and have his sleep in the afternoon instead!

Fear is the Spur

By William Armstrong

'Pull in!' I said suddenly. 'There. Just at that gate.'

Nigel, our son-in-law, edged the big Land Rover onto the grass verge of the narrow country road and drew to a halt. He turned and looked at me inquiringly. 'What...?'

'Leave it.' I cut in tersely, easing my eighty-year-old arthritic frame out of the front seat. 'I've waited some sixty-three years for this moment. Don't spoil it now.'

Stiffly, I made my way over to the wide iron gate. Progress, I sneered to myself. What happened to the old rural crafts, when gates were made of seasoned timber and you could carve your initials on them? Behind me I heard the murmur of voices in the Land Rover.

'...getting worse with his 'down memory lane' stunts.' That was Morag, our elder daughter; feisty as ever. 'What's he looking for anyway?'

'His youth.' I smiled at Jean's quiet rejoinder to Morag's abrasive remark. During the fifty years we'd been married I'd never once heard her voice raised to any of the family, and yet they all knew that line they couldn't cross. 'Something happened in that field which changed him forever. Of course he never talks about it. Maybe, now he's been here, it'll lay whatever ghost is there. Let's hope so anyway.'

I grinned wryly to myself as I gazed across the sixty-acre field to the wood extending down the far side. Beyond the wood, partially screened from my view, were the cottages and the farm buildings which had played such a prominent part in my youthful development.

Standing there, staring with unseeing eyes at the rolling Border countryside, I was no longer eighty-year-old James Anderson, retired local government officer and respected Church of Scotland elder. Instead I was Jim Anderson, seventeen, who could run like a deer, and was hopelessly smitten by Mary McKinnon, landgirl and local 'femme fatale'. The spring sky was blue, with fleecy white clouds drifting lazily across it, but I didn't notice. Way back in my memory the scene had changed to a gathering storm, with thunder rumbling overhead and lightning flashing incessantly. And, transcending all else, was that gut wrenching, heart stopping fear that had gripped me all those years long ago.

Because fear is something I've lived with all my life. When I was small it was a fear of dogs. Farm collies in particular. The kind that feigned disinterest, while slinking in behind you with the explicit intention of nipping the back of your leg. Second only to collies were foxhounds. I didn't mind so much when they were trotting past on their way to a meet, with the huntsman at their head and the whipper-in close up behind. No; it was when I heard that rolling clarion call of the pack in full cry, and I knew that on my two mile walk home from our little country school I would almost certainly meet them, that fear used to grip me. It wasn't entirely unfounded. Way back in local hunting lore was the story of the rogue pack with, it was said, a trace of bloodhound in them, who had hunted the high Cheviot valleys. It was rumoured that they weren't averse to swinging off their pursuit of Reynard onto the track of sundry small children, and that several nasty incidents had only been averted by the alertness of the huntsman and his whipper-in.

Gradually however, as I got older, my fear of dogs faded somewhat, though I would never describe myself as a dog lover. We maintained an attitude of armed neutrality towards each other.

But fear stayed with me in other forms. It was as though I couldn't function properly without it. And, to a certain extent, that was true. All through my life I've taken risks, driven on by the spur of fear. And on every occasion, after it was all over, I've sneered at myself. 'You fool, why couldn't you just admit you were afraid?' But I couldn't. The fear of admission was greater than the physical fear itself. Standing there, looking back down the years, I could just imagine what Mary McKinnon's reaction would have been if I'd admitted to my fear. Her look of scorn. 'Away, you big Jessie!' And I desperately wanted to look good in her eyes. Those same dark eyes which could reduce me to putty with a glance.

All those fears were unusual in a country boy, and they were cranked up by my vivid imagination. At least, that's what my father said. Maybe he had a point. 'You read too many damned books!' was his, scathing pronouncement. But then, fear of dogs or bulls never bothered him.

Because I was very afraid of bulls. It all began at the tender age of six, when I was on my way home from school one spring evening. I came upon a red Shorthorn bull steadily reducing a stout five-barred gate to matchwood. Fear lends you wings so they say, and certainly that evening I produced a terrific turn of speed. Rushing home I blurted out my story and then watched, wide-eyed, from an upstairs window, as the bull was rounded up and incarcerated in one of the cattle courts until he cooled down.

I'd hoped to become a joiner, but the war intervened and I found myself working on a large farm in the Scottish Borders. Fortunately, during this period I was involved with horses and tractors, and had only fleeting contact with bulls. Carting straw into the cattle courts for bedding, or feeding stock which were being outwintered pretty well covered it, and in those situations the bulls were either well fed and sleepy, or cold and hungry. In neither case were they looking for trouble.

But Nemesis waits for everyone and never more so than on a farm. The year had moved on, with spring picking up speed and heading towards summer. Now, the stables which had been the focal point of the farm life were suddenly unoccupied. The horses were turned out to pasture and there they stayed until late August, or early September, only being brought in when required.

There was quite a ritual to all this. Big John, the farm grieve or foreman; an august personage with a penchant for chewing tobacco, would stop beside you on the afternoon of the previous day, hose a stream of tobacco juice from the corner of his mouth, look into the distance and mutter gruffly; 'Catch a horse the morn an' yoke the scraper in the Steelbrae.' This meant you'd be cultivating between the rows of swedes in the field known as Steelbrae.

Bright and early next morning you made your way to where your team was being pastured, or 'rinnin' at the gress' as it was more colloquially known. In addition to a leather or rope halter, you also carried a small quantity of oats as a bait, while you slipped the halter onto the chosen horse. This was necessary because some horses were notoriously 'bad catchers', and would go to considerable lengths to avoid being caught.

Having been brought in, the horses were given a feed of grain, while you went home for a belated breakfast prior to starting work.

Where possible, the draught horses would be pastured in fields close to the farm steading. Occasionally there might be a bull in the same field, but this was rare. The breeding cattle were usually held on an outlying part of the farm.

To date I'd been lucky and, at the time in question, my team, a big placid bay gelding and a longstriding temperamental roan mare, were running in a sixty acre field about a quarter of a mile from the steading. No great distance in itself, but a field that size, which sloped upwards to a ridge, with hollows on the other side, meant that you sometimes had to do a fair bit of walking and checking before you found the horses. The only other occupants of the pasture were a sizeable flock of sheep and twenty Aberdeen Angus heifers. No problems.

Summer had arrived in all its glory when trouble finally caught up with me. I was helping the local blacksmith get the mowers ready for the hay season, when a large cattle float lumbered into the steading.

Within minutes, Dave Johnston, the cattleman, had appeared from the barn with old Shep, his collie, tagging along behind. 'Aye,' I heard him say to the lorry driver; 'this'll be the new Angus bull the boss has juist bocht. Back up an' we'll rin'm intae that close,' indicating one of the empty cattle courts. 'Jim,' to me, 'gies a hand tae open thae doors.'

As Dave and I struggled to get the doors open the driver manoeuvred the big Albion float into position.

Five minutes later, with the cattle court doors open, the lorry ramp down and its side fencing in position, everything was ready. 'Right,' Dave nodded to the driver. 'Let'm oot.'

Climbing up the sides of the float the driver slipped the catches on the rear doors and threw them back. Then he banged on the slatted side. There was a rumbling snort from the interior of the float and the bull materialised suddenly in the opening.

I had just time to note a massive head and a pair of baleful red-rimmed eyes, then he was down the ramp with a rush and standing in the middle of the court tossing straw in all directions.

At close quarters he was an impressive package of black rippling muscle and latent power. 'Man,' Dave said as we closed the doors, 'he's a bit nippy on his feet, this yin. We'll need tae watch'm. Onywey,' he added, shredding tobacco between leathery palms and tamping it into his pipe, 'he's gaun tae the Mosspark the morn.'

The Mosspark! An icy feeling crawled up my spine. That was where my team was.

'Aye,' added Dave in answer to my unspoken question. 'The boss is gaun tae breed pure Aberdeen Angus stock.'

How Dave got the bull to the Mosspark the next day I don't know. Most likely, Peter, the shepherd, lent a hand and they boxed him in with several collies. Suffice to say I saw the heifers milling about and I knew, without being told, that he was there. Sooner or later I would have to face my Nemesis.

For several days nothing happened. We were in the middle of turnip thinning and horse work was minimal. Then, during Saturday morning, the blow fell. Big John materialised at my elbow as I was scything nettles in the stackyard. 'Jim.' The tobacco juice just missed my boots. 'Catch a horse on Monday mornin' an' yoke the scraper in the Westflat.' And with that he was gone.

'Well,' I thought, 'that's it. Suppose it had to happen sooner or later.'

The weekend was hot and sultry. Earlier in the week I'd persuaded Mary McKinnon that the cinema in the local town was showing a good film, so why not come with me to see it. Mary knew I was desperate for a date with her and, while I didn't rate very highly in the league of local talent, nevertheless a free evening wasn't to be sneezed at. I'd been looking forward to the date all week, particularly the prospect of getting Mary alone on the return journey. If all stories were true she was hot stuff, and I was keen to find out.

Until Big John and his damned 'catch a horse' routine came along. All through the film, try as I might, I couldn't get the bull out of my mind. My response to Mary's attempts to snuggle up to me in the back seats was, at best, half-hearted. So much so that she eventually gave up and settled down to watch the film, at the same time working her way through the box of chocolates I'd bought her earlier in the evening.

The run home wasn't much better. Our conversation was desultory to say the least. However, when we came to the last mile, a gentle downhill run all the way to the farm, Mary grudgingly agreed to stop at a convenient gate. We were just getting into a very satisfying clinch, and I was beginning to think that the evening hadn't been entirely wasted when, across the valley, that bloody new bull started bellowing. The high soprano blare of a bull that is angry and wants the whole world to know about it.

I'd just succeeded in unhooking Mary's bra and the sound stopped me dead. 'Go on,' Mary said softly, 'I don't mind.' It appeared that all those stories I'd heard recounted with such relish were true.

But I couldn't. No way. I stood there in a fumbling trance, while the bull bellowed his anger at the night.

'Forget it!' Mary said angrily, fastening her bra. 'You've had your chance. That's the last time I go out wi' you, Jim Anderson.' Together we mounted our bikes and rode the rest of the way home in stony silence.

Sunday I got up late and, feeling frustrated as only a teenage youth with rampant hormones can, had breakfast and decided to go for a walk. Somehow

I gravitated towards the Mosspark and I found myself walking the old farm road which ran along the bottom of the field. 'Assuming I can get the horses within striking distance of the fence' I ruminated, 'I've got an escape route if I need it.' Glancing up I saw the bull silhouetted on the crest of the ridge. There was something sinister in the way the massive head swivelled as he watched me pacing along the road. 'Well,' I thought grimly; Monday will tell.' It was a warm summer morning but I shivered involuntarily.

That night I slept badly and rose early on Monday morning. There was an oppressive feeling in the air. Thunder rumbled in the distance, came closer and then receded inconclusively. A storm was brewing.

Collecting a halter and some grain from the stable from the stable, I headed for Mosspark. The mare, I knew, would be excited and nervous. She hated thunderstorms. However, big Prince, the gelding, was a placid animal, and might just be waiting for me at the gate.

No such luck. Mosspark stretched before me, seemingly devoid of all life. 'Damn,' I thought, peering upfield into the gathering gloom, lit by periodic flashes of lightning. 'I bet they're all bunched in the hollows behind the ridge. Anyway, I'll walk along the bottom road and up the far side in case I've missed them in the bad light.'

Self justification which got me precisely nowhere. I was badly scared and I knew it.

By now the lightning was flashing almost continuously, while the thunder seemed to be ripping the heavens apart directly overhead. At the same time the first drops of rain struck my face as I peered through the gathering gloom. There was nothing in that corner of the field, and I knew with a cold numbing certainty that they were all; horses, cattle and sheep, bunched behind the ridge.

'Well, there's no help for it,' I thought grimly as I started up the slope, parallel with the fence and some twenty yards infield. By now the rain was really getting into its stride.

Suddenly a vivid flash lit up the field and there, pacing menacingly down the slope towards me was my Nemesis, the bull. Head lowered, massive shoulders hunched, and a hoarse rumble rising and falling in his throat, he looked like something out of a nightmare.

For a split second fear, cold paralysing fear, laid a clammy hand on my shoulder, then suddenly it was gone and I was gripped by a raging berserk fury. For days this damned animal had monopolised my thoughts during working hours and had put a crimp in my personal life, and now, on top of all that I had the thunderstorm and the missing horses to contend with.

Swinging the halter round my head I let out a wild yell and raced towards the bull. For a heartstopping second he stood his ground, then he turned and ran! I can remember cursing with fury as I lashed his hindquarters with the halter rope. Me; James Anderson, who in later years would look askance at anyone who used profanity. Together we raced some hundred yards before he outdistanced me and I stopped, exhausted.

But the bull didn't stop. Oh no! He'd had a shock he wouldn't forget in a hurry. I stood there, chest heaving, gulping in air, as I watched him racing for the shelter of the wood on the far side of the field.

Suddenly it hit me. I was free. Free of the nagging shaming fear I'd hidden all these years. There was a whinny and I turned to see Prince, the bay gelding, trotting down the slope. 'Well, boy,' I said as I buckled on the halter while he champed on a mouthful of grain; 'I'll never worry again when Big John says 'catch a....' The storm dissolved into a blue spring sky as the discordant note of the horn cut through my thoughts. Morag beckoned impatiently.

Stiffly, I made my way back to the Land Rover and climbed in. 'Thought you'd fallen asleep, Dad.' That was Morag; as usual. 'We've got lunch booked in Kelso.'

Nigel looked at me quizzically. 'Find what you were looking for?'

'Yes,' I said, mentally consigning Mary McKinnon; Mary of the flashing dark eyes and the impressive bosom, to history. I sensed Jean was waiting intently for my reply. 'What you have is better than what you never had. Let's go.'

Image Taker

By David Cruikshanks

Edward dragged back the yellow patterned curtains and blinked at the day-light, his thin lips curling up into a smile. His gnarled hands shook a little as he fumbled for the tiebacks, before hooking them into place.

He stared out at the sandstone tenement, separated from him by a thick pane of glass. A young man in a suit peered in and locked onto Edward's gaze framed in the window, before continuing his relentless march to work. The traffic roared by but Edward's room was bathed in silence as well as light. He let out a contented sigh. Time for reading and contemplation and hours of staring at his beloved paintings. He turned to greet the thick square frame enclosing an explosion of violent brush strokes and visceral colours. His bony fingers stretched upwards, straining to trace the wrinkly lines around the thick paint of his favourite picture, a portrait by Paul Hewson. The man in the pic-ture, probably a drunk picked up by the artist, was red in the face through too much drink or anger or perhaps a mixture. The green shoots of Edward's mind sprang up and he fantasised that the portrait could be of a high flying execu-tive, brutalised by endless office hours and meaningless meetings followed by evenings boozing and chasing women, a toll that had probably ended in tears and nights spent in cardboard boxes.

Edward's thought train was broken by a knock at his bedroom door. The jolly, slightly plump nurse bellowed the arrival of a visitor. It was the photogra-pher, despatched by some vaguely fashionable magazine to record the ephem-era that made up his life, a collection of works known as literature. That was what he was made up of. That was how the media's gospel to the outside world portrayed him. Well, he would play the game a few more times, after all, it was for a good cause.

He sat up straight in his wheel chair and held out a beckoning hand. The tall, strapping slightly nervy photographer bent down and took it, although he never looked directly at Edward when he said hello. Edward thought that his bearing leant more to the shipyards than photography and immediately chastised himself for such snobbery. He had a lot of kit this lad, most of it black and dull, probably made from some indestructible material.

Edward had done this many times before. He listened to the photographer's banal musings on the weather, How long Edward had been here? Did he like it? What made a poem? What did he think of the Scots Parliament? Edward provided the photographer with suitable answers he thought. Yes he agreed that the weather was nice, oh he quite enjoyed living in a nursing home. He wished the Scottish Parliament would now put substance over style, that kind of thing. The photographer muddled about a bit more. He insisted on putting up a large sheet as a background, covering his favourite painting, but then he didn't seem to use it. As the shoot progressed, the photographer seemed to relax, perhaps he had captured what he wanted from Edward so he too began to enjoy himself. It had been a few months, maybe a year, since anyone had wanted to take his picture. Twenty years ago, they were queuing at the door to the University. He only had to dash off a letter to the papers about something or other and they practically camped outside his office.

Since the onset of his cancer, things had quietened down. He had left his mansion block in the West End for the more modest trappings of a nursing home further east, in a slightly downbeat part of the city.

The constant visits to his home by artists, writers and thinkers had been replaced by a drip, drip of well-wishers at his modest room in the nursing home, he hated the word hospice, it smacked of do-gooding. What had mattered to him most was that he was able to bring his art collection to the home. The supervisor was delighted to receive such a celebrity resident and promptly let the papers know all about life with Scotland's most famous living writer.

Edward didn't mind one bit, after all, he wasn't exactly engaged in three in the bed romps with the nursing staff.

Every morning he rose to inspect his paintings. He had wanted to become an artist once, dabbling with it before succumbing to the written word, well it seemed to come more easily to him. There was that one chance to go to the art school but 'what's life without a few regrets?' he consoled himself.

He would miss his collection of paintings by some of Scotland's most celebrated artists that's for sure but 'you can't take them with you' was his stock answer. He had decided to donate them to the local museum and when he saw the joy on the curator's face he wished he had done so years ago. When probed by a journalist on one of the tabloids if he was perhaps 'mad not to sell them?' he replied 'And buy what with the money? Two coffins?' The journalist shrank back at this retort and shuffled on to do a judge and stripper story instead.

'That's me then.'

'What, oh yes, sorry I was miles away there, what did you say?'

'That's me finished, nae bother ah'll see ma sel' oot nae need tae get up. An' thanks pal, thanks fur everything.'

'Don't mention it, it was nice to meet you.' Edward said. He thought he might have dozed off in a daydream but it was probably the medication.

'Well goodbye then, I didn't catch your name.'

'That's awright mate dinnae worry aboot it, see ye.'

Edward sat puzzled as the photographer sprinted out of the doorway, bashing his equipment against the wall. He had left a tripod on the floor and Edward buzzed the staff to let them know.

A few minutes later Robin, the plump nurse arrived with a cup of tea.

'How did it go then Edward?' Robin enquired, bouncing the pitch of the words up and down as if asking a toddler how he had enjoyed his first day at nursery.

Edward replied 'Very well thanks, Robin, thanks for the tea.'

Robin sat quietly, waiting for more information but Edward munched his Garibaldi biscuit and slurped the hot tea without another word.

'Well I must be going,' announced Robin, 'must get lunch ready.'

'Oh okay then, see you at lunch' Edward replied. Edward liked his little games with Robin, sometimes he would divulge tit-bits of gossip but Robin had started taking root in Edward's room which had disturbed his writing, so now he fed him information piecemeal with the promise that if he left now there would be another juicy instalment at a later date.

The door snapped behind Robin and Edward smiled. He turned his wheel chair around to his typewriter and flexed his hands cracking some of the bony fingers. Yes he would miss his paintings but they would fill a huge hole in the museum's collection and anyway, he could visualise them in his mind everytime he closed his eyes.

He looked up at the Hewson but where its solid frame had housed the masterpiece there was a one foot square of faded magnolia plasterboard. In the middle of the plasterboard a picture hook stuck out. On the end of the hook the wrinkled husk of a spider clutched around a worn out web.

He closed his eyes and prayed. Then, opening them, he stared at the plaster-board square but nothing happened. He closed his eyes once more, this time he didn't pray. He opened his eyes but the same plasterboard square stared back at him. He reached for the call buzzer but the intercom barked back at him before he had a chance to press it.

A voice filled with consternation echoed around his bedroom

'Mr Morrison, another photographer has arrived and insists that he has an appointment with you.'

Edward closed his eyes and laughed.

'Send him in Edna, oh and Edna?'

'Yes Mr. Morrison'

'Phone the museum and tell them I've decided to keep the Hewson.'

Tell Love it is but Lust

By Anne Ewing

There was trouble in the parish and it was growing worse, gradually but inexorably, week by week. Privately expressed doubts, exchanged "sotto voce" after Sunday services, and whispered concerns shared in clandestine phone calls, were beginning to escalate into tentative signs of overt discontent at the Kirk Session and the Women's Guild. The source of all this angst were the recently inducted minister and his wife, Duncan McFarquhar and Gwendoline Heathcote-Ampleforth. (The printing bill for new church stationery was the cause of the first of the raised eyebrows!). There was a general feeling that a young man with a family would be a refreshing change after nearly forty years of selfless but, it had to be said, increasingly ineffectual service by old Reverend Johnston and his timid mouse of a wife. The arrival of these colourful and flamboyant cats amongst the insipid and humdrum pigeons of the parish resulted initially in a stunned and bewildered tolerance, gradually developed into genuine concern and was now well on the way to becoming scandalised outrage and downright animosity.

Duncan was a son of the manse, the product of emotionally sterile parents and a loveless home, who couldn't believe his luck when he met Gwennie as he started his divinity degree at university. Her background was completely different from Duncan's. Her father's family was of the impoverished gentry, while her mother had had fleeting success on the west-end stage before the war. They now enjoyed an eccentric and precarious lifestyle somewhere in the Home Counties. After graduation, the young couple married immediately, without the approval of either set of parents and spent some years in the World Missions in various parts of Africa and the Far East, where they felt called to administer spiritual and educational enlightenment to some of Jock Tamson's bairns there, before returning to Scotland to take up their first pastoral charge.

By then they had three little boys, who, it was noted in the village, were remarkably unalike for brothers, one dark with almond shaped eyes, one blonde and blue-eyed and the third red-haired and freckled. These "braw bairns fu'o' life" had soon become "impident wee deevils". There was some concern that what was good enough for the children of the parishioners was not good enough for them, as their parents opted for home schooling. This seemed to involve a lot of running wild in the manse garden and causing havoc in the churchyard. Tam, the beadle, whose tenure in his post had lasted almost as long as the previous incumbents in the parish, privately thought that each of the boys "wid be nane the waur fur a guid skelp on the lug", and would have been only too happy to oblige, given half a chance.

While the Kirk Session was prepared to accept some innovation in the areas of doctrine and methodology, they found some of the new minister's changes unsettling and uncomfortable. His introduction of the reciting of the Apostle's creed and some congregational responses in prayers were tolerated, but kneeling for the blessing during the sacraments caused some consternation amongst the strictest adherents to the Presbyterian way of doing things amongst his flock, despite what the General Assembly said about ecumenism. The greatest disappointment came, however in his choice of hymns where many old favourites were abandoned in favour of the more "happy-clappy" songs of praise, especially when he and his young wife insisted on accompanying the singing on guitar and sitar respectively. The first time this happened, the congregation left the church almost visibly reeling with shock. His sermons were usually based on obscure tenets of theology intellectually beyond the ken of most of his listeners, and pandrops were sooked with more than usual desperation as he strove to remain politically correct in all his declamations. The boredom quotient had never been higher, not even when old Johnston had succumbed to a degree of mental confusion, and rambled on in barely audible whispers.

The manse was a sprawling old house, riddled with damp and in great need of complete renovation, but some volunteers amongst the congregation had done what they could with woodchip and emulsion to make the place look better. They were consequently rather miffed when they noticed that those same walls had been swathed in all manner of exotic—and in some cases erotic—wall hangings and posters while the sober and sensible light fittings had been replaced with huge paper shades in a rainbow of colours. Similarly, the front garden of the manse, which some of the keen gardeners in the parish had laid with a new lawn and some pretty flower beds, had been dug up by the minister's wife and replaced with a herb garden, including large clumps of tall leafy plants which none of the locals could identify. In this enterprise she had enlisted the enthusiastic assistance of a young, itinerant labourer of the district, described by her as a "free spirit", but referred to by others as a "coorse tink". They could often be seen and heard, laughing and chatting together in the garden and the old ramshackle green house.

This was not the kind of behaviour that was expected of a minister's wife, but then neither was her appearance. She usually wore rather low cut, sleeveless vests and long flowing skirts. She favoured long dangly earrings and lots of beads, her legs were bare in all weathers and the only footwear she seemed to possess were open sandals. "That lassie'll catch 'er daith o' cauld gaun aboot like that," was the opinion of some of the older ladies, whose outrage grew even more vocal when they noticed that the sight of the young woman cycling merrily around the parish seemed to bring an unaccustomed twinkle to the eye of some of their menfolk.

She was also creating some confusion and misunderstanding in her dealings with the Women's Guild in the matter of planning their syllabus for the year's meetings. She had invited the owner of the health food shop in the neighbouring town to come and talk about alternative therapies and remedies, most of which were regarded with grave mistrust. "Echinacea and garlic tablets? No way! I'll stick to my good old kaolin poultice!" They were even more appalled when they realised that the minister's wife was processing potions and powders from her own plants and herbs, which to some, reeked of witchcraft and cauldrons. Old Mrs Anderson who was very hard of hearing was completely bewildered when she heard there would soon be a talk about a "feminine tractor with a German gear". She was a farmer's daughter herself and had driven a tractor many times, but always thought there was only one gender, and any way surely that would have been a more appropriate topic for the Men's Club meetings. However, being very sensitive about her hearing loss and determined not to have to resort to a hearing aid, she kept quiet about the whole prospect. Another insult came as some of the ladies were deeply hurt when their home baking, in which they took justified pride, was eschewed in favour of the young interloper's pro-biotic and whole-food tray bakes at the coffee mornings in the church hall.

Duncan himself had begun to feel that the promising start he had made in his new charge had somehow begun to stall, and he was concerned that his flock were not responding to him as positively as he had hoped. He prided himself on being sensitive to their needs and was prepared to try a different tack if need be. In addition, he was vaguely aware that the enthusiasm with which his wife approached her parish duties was not exactly helping her to make friends and influence people. He had long suspected that she had often taken the instruction to "love thy neighbour" somewhat too literally. Nevertheless, he was very disappointed and indeed, saddened when she came to him in a very agitated state one Saturday morning, reporting that her precious and much loved bicycle had been stolen. In its place by the back door of the manse she had found a pair of very old and disreputable looking brown leather walking shoes. Was someone trying to tell her something? Did the parishioners think it unseemly for her to cycle and should she be walking around the place instead? "What can it mean, Dearheart?" she pleaded with her husband. He had no immediate answer, but as he settled down later to prepare his sermon for the next day, it came to him that perhaps he should try a change of tactics with his congregation. After all, they had been used to a more traditional kind of pastor, and perhaps they would respond to a firmer hand and a bit of old fashioned fire and brimstone. So he called his wife into his study and suggested a ploy to shame the bicycle thief and at the same time show that he was not a minister to be trifled with. Tomorrow morning he would deliver a sermon on the Seven Deadly Sins. He would stress the dreadful retribution that would await anyone who indulged in wrath, sloth, envy, gluttony, lust, pride or greed. By the time he arrived at the last of the sins, he was certain that the person who had succumbed to the pride of avarice, to the extent of stealing his dear wife's bicycle, would give themselves away. "We must watch everyone closely Gwennie, and I am sure you will see some sign of guilt or discomfort on the face of the culprit. Perhaps they will blush with shame or shift restlessly in their seats, but I am sure in some way we will be able to tell who the sinner is. Then we can speak privately to them and counsel them to expunge their sin and at the very least get your bike back."

So the plot was hatched and as the time for the sermon drew near, Gwendoline readied herself to scan the faces of the congregation. Duncan started in his usual diffident and gentle manner, but gradually began to get into his stride. By the time he got to the sin of envy he was actually waving his arms about and raising his voice to the extent that many of his listeners seemed to sit up and take notice of what he was saying, as they exchanged glances with each other. "This is more like it!" they seemed to be thinking. As he reached the sin of lust he had built up such a head of steam that it seemed his audience was almost about to burst into applause. As he paused for breath before tackling pride, he was stunned to see Gwendoline suddenly rush out of her seat in the gallery and with a swish of her skirt and a flash of her braceleted ankle, disappear out of the door. He faltered as he tried to continue his tirade, but somehow he had lost the concentration necessary to sustain the earlier impetus. As he reached the climax and objective of the sermon, his voice had lost its fiery pitch and he finished off in his usual reasonable and measured style. He even forgot to look for signs of guilt in his congregation, as they resumed their normal bored expressions, fortified in many cases by one last surreptitious pandrop.

It was more than two hours later, as he prepared the four-bean stew, their normal late Sunday lunch, and the boys were causing their usual mayhem, when Gwendoline appeared. She seemed flushed and breathless as she sallied into the kitchen.

"Darling, where did you go? You missed the end of my sermon. Now we'll never know who stole your bike!"

"But yes, Sweetness", she reassured him, "I have got it back. Your plan worked perfectly, you clever boy."

She swept across the room and showered Duncan with kisses. Holding his head between her hands, she explained, "You see, as soon as you started to talk about lust, I remembered exactly where I left my bicycle!"

As Duncan stood there with a dazed and perplexed expression on his face, she turned and lifted her copy of "The Female Eunuch", undoubtedly her favourite feminist tract, from the kitchen table and gushed, "Now I simply must get on with my talk to the Women's Guild, I am sure they will be so impressed with Germaine Greer. When will lunch be ready, Petal?"

The Balloon Man and the Pretty Woman

By William Clinkenbeard

People appeared to approach him in two quite different ways: they got there either by an excited child dragging a reluctant parent by the hand, or by an eager parent pushing a fearful child out in front. Either way, the Balloon Man received them gladly. He stood, feet firmly planted, in the middle of a wide pedestrian area just beyond the wrought-iron fence enclosing the outside tables of the restaurant. We had just finished dinner and were polishing off a bottle of wine in the warm summer evening, so it was pleasant just to sit and observe. The Balloon Man had an absurd red and yellow balloon hat jammed onto his head and a multi-pocketed apron around his waist holding a fresh supply of balloons plus his required tools and fixings.

On this street at dusk he was the main attraction, but not the only one. In the children's' play area in the park, parents pushed their kids on swings and roundabouts to piercing squeals of delight. A few yards down from the restaurant a street fountain threw up vertical jets of water in random sequence. While adults stood around trying to figure out the sophisticated fountain mechanics, their children were simply enjoying it, hopping around to catch a jet with their foot as it erupted or throwing their balloons hopefully. The jets possessed an uncanny ability to locate the balloons and punch them higher into the air. A weird and wonderful assortment of trikes, pushchairs and bikes paraded through the area, including a unicycle pedalled uncertainly by an Abraham Lincoln look-alike in a top hat. Strings of lights strewn through leafy trees completed the surreal nature of the scene. At the edge of town and dominating it, Aspen Mountain rose ominously in the fading light. This was Aspen, Colorado, home of the summer music festival, playground of the rich and famous: a mountainous vault containing more intellectual capital than any-where else in the United States, but leaking eccentricity.

The Balloon Man fashioned whatever the child or parent requested: a pirate's sword, a crazy hat, a stick figure, or a dachshund dog. The fresh balloons were extracted from his pocket, quickly blown up, tied and then twisted and woven into realistic shapes. The easy art of it made compelling viewing. But the hushed conversations he held with child and parent were even more intriguing. What could he possibly be conveying in these lengthy conversations? He worked almost faster than the eye could see, but then stood and talked. How much *could* be said about the fabrication of a sword or crazy hat? Was he apologising to ethically-sensitive parents for making their child a weapon of war or was he giving them advice on how to care for their new balloon dog? How could this be a profitable exercise for him when the working time taken for each piece was extended to five or even ten minutes by conversation, finally to be rewarded by only a dollar or two? The man sometimes went on talking to a parent long after the children were flashing their swords and were duelling fiercely in the street. We observed all this quietly from our table, not appreciating that the very next day would provide an answer, albeit an enigmatic one.Saturday began wet and looked like staying wet for the rest of the day. Only the foot of Aspen Mountain could be seen at the edge of the town. The legs and trunk and head were rendered invisible by cloud and rain. No one was interested in riding the chairlift, even at greatly reduced prices. Sports Utility Vehicles circled round the streets, letting passengers disgorge, dive into shops through the rain and then dive out again. A heavy, wet blanket had been thrown over the town.

Refuge was taken in Starbuck's Coffee, where, curiously, the Balloon Man had also taken up position. Another long and earnest conversation was being carried out over coffee with a young mum whose curly-headed daughter sported a futuristic balloon hat. What could the man be talking about for so long? When mother and daughter had departed, a greeting and a word of praise from us soon unlocked the door.

'They don't like me much,' he said. 'Aspen isn't too bad, but some other towns are terrible. They don't want you doing balloons outside their shops and restaurants.' 'Who doesn't?' we asked, not believing that anyone could possibly find fault with a man who provided such innocent and enthralling entertainment.

'The people in charge of things, the town authorities. Do you know that yesterday I went into the Hotel Jerome and sat down, just to rest? I was only sitting there and the manager came along to move me off. They don't want you in there unless you're a paying guest.'

'But surely,' we offered, 'you are drawing customers to the place, to the shops and restaurants. You're increasing their business.'

'Yes,' he said, 'but they still resent me. They're only interested in money, and they imagine that I'm taking it away from them. They're all racketeers. I've been moved off the street all over the country. I've been arrested and in jail so many times. By the way, where are you from? I hear an accent.'

'Scotland,' we said.

'I know Scotland,' he said. 'I've been in the tank in Glasgow. Terrible place. I like Glasgow, but the jail is awful. I didn't have the right papers or something when I got there. I was lucky to get out. Where do you go in this country?'

'Scottsdale, Arizona,' we said. 'We have a little place there.'

'I've been to Scottsdale,' he said. 'In fact, I got arrested there too. They took me in for doing balloons without a license. But then I discovered that the sheriff had no legal right to arrest me. I got a lawyer and threatened to sue him, and he had to let me out. It cost me, but at least I got away. Hey, do you know Julia Roberts?'

We said that we did. I volunteered that she was a great looker, especially in jeans. My wife glowered at me.

'We've just seen her in *Erin Brockovich*,' I said. 'Have you seen it?'

'No,' said the Balloon Man. 'I haven't seen it yet, but she was great in *Pretty Woman*. She's a friend of mine, you know. She has a house here. She had this big party and sent a car into town to pick me up. She'd seen me doing my balloons in town. I talked to her a lot at the party and she likes me. In fact, I'm writing a script for a movie for her. I've got these puppets at home, see. I make them myself because I'm really a puppeteer. So I'm writing this script starring Julia Roberts along with my puppets. She's very interested in it. When some of those hangers-on of hers started getting at me, she just told them to lay off. She's really great.'

The Balloon Man began to tell us in detail about the script. There was a long and complicated description of the plot and the characters and the action.

'After I sent them the script,' he said, 'they kept calling me from Hollywood. Every day for a while, I got calls wanting to know about this and that. I hope that the film will be made soon. I've got my puppets all ready to go.'

'It sounds great,' we said. 'Julia Roberts must be grateful to you. The screenplay sounds so creative and imaginative, and it could be a wonderful opportunity for you. It could really make your name. We'll look forward to seeing it. What name should we look for in the credits?'

He paused for a few moments. 'Oh, he said, 'I don't think my name will appear in the credits. They wouldn't allow that. Just look for *The Balloon Man.*'

The Reluctant Revolutionary

By William Armstrong

The long-stemmed table lamp cast a soft pool of light over the massive mahogany leather-topped desk, leaving the remainder of the room in shadow. It highlighted the bronzed features of the man leaning forward in the big chair, brow furrowed in concentration as he scanned the document in front of him.

Scrutiny completed, Juan de Liberio, President of the state of Parador, nodded. Everything was in order. Face set in harsh lines, de Liberio appended his signature. The death sentence he had just signed gave him no pleasure, but it was necessary.

Someone knocked discreetly.

'Come.'

The soldier who entered the room was slim, of medium build, and with the swarthy good looks of a Latin American. He affected a pencil thin moustache, and his jet black hair was carefully styled. His immaculate, well-cut, olive-green uniform, was obviously modelled on British Army equipment. This was hardly surprising. Colonel Ramon D'Inzencio was a fanatical Anglophile. In addition, he idolised the president. Way back in the heady days of the revolution they had fought together, and the man behind the desk had saved his life. That day the skinny fifteen-year-old, who was later to become Colonel D'Inzencio, had sworn a silent oath that, as long as he drew breath, no harm would come to the big Englishman.

Now, he came smartly to attention and saluted.

'At ease, Ramon.' The president's expression softened as he looked up at his young aide. 'Everything is ready?'

'Yes, Excellency. He has been visited by the priest, and has received absolution. Commandante Hernandez has alerted the firing squad and they are standing by. I will read the statement to the press afterwards.' He stopped

- 130 -

abruptly, uncomfortably aware, as always, of the piercing stare from the cold blue eyes.

'You have done well.…He is the first for some time. There will be many complaints when the world hears of his execution.'

'Excellency, everyone knows that the penalty for bringing drugs, or arms, into Parador, is death. You made these laws and they have served us well.'

'True.' De Liberio rose quickly, his huge figure dwarfing the slim colonel. Six feet six, and built in proportion, the bearded president seemed even larger in the shadowy room. A youthful fifty-year-old, he still moved with an easy grace. Dressed as usual in his working garb of green fatigues and open-necked shirt, it was easy to picture the great guerrilla fighter he had once been. 'Unfortunately, the world does not see it that way. They say that such laws are barbaric, even though they have kept our country free of guns and drugs all those years.'

The dapper colonel drew himself up proudly. 'Then the world is foolish, Excellency. One has only to travel through Parador to see how it has prospered under your rule.'

'Thank you, Ramon.' A massive hand descended on D'Inzencio's shoulder. 'You are my right arm.' The president proffered a sheet of papers. 'Here is the decree for the execution. See that it is delivered to Commandante Hernandez. Also the statement for the press afterwards. And I have explained personally to the British ambassador that my decision stands. I understand the young man has no family?'

'That is correct. It seems he was an only child and his parents are both dead.'

The president frowned. 'I regret this,' he said heavily. 'However, as you say, there can be no exceptions. Executions are never pleasant, but they are part of the price we must pay to keep Parador safe. Go now.' He raised a hand in dismissal.

'At once, Exellency.' The dapper colonel came smartly to attention and saluted. A salute which was returned immediately. His Excellency was a stickler for protocol. Turning smartly, Colonel Ramon D'Incenzio, Controller of the Presidential Guard, and personal aide to Presidente Juan de Liberio, strode from the room.

A good man, the president mused. He's almost ready. Some day, he reflected, leaning back in the big chair, he'll sit behind this desk and I'll be able to retire. Have I done enough to exorcise my demons? The demons that have driven me all those years. I wonder? At least, John Strange, ex-SAS captain; alias John Sanderson, arms dealer; alias Juan de Liberio, President of Parador, you tried.

Pain stabbed suddenly above his right eye, and he shook his head angrily, like a goaded bull. These pains were becoming more frequent lately. Doctor Garcia had warned him that additional tests were needed, but Garcia was like an old woman where El Presidente's health was concerned. It was probably nothing more than a migraine. Anyway; he reached into a drawer, there were always painkillers.

Eyes closed, waiting for the pill to take effect, John Strange reflected on the irony of his position, remembering once again that little sun baked fort in the desert. 'A nest of vipers,' Colonel Prescott had called it. 'Pity it's across the border. Of course,' the CO's left eyelid had drooped fractionally, 'if someone was to mount a night raid.... Just a thought. Now, about those new training schedules....'

Nothing more was said, but it had been enough. He'd sounded out the boys and they'd been all for it. A quick job and no questions asked.

And so it proved. He remembered the surge of adrenaline as they scaled the crumbling walls. The short vicious firefight, which ended with all the ragtag garrison either dead or captive, and the squad, thankfully, with only a few minor flesh wounds.

It was then he'd made the decision to kill the prisoners and blow up the fort. The boys had agreed, especially when he said he'd do the killing himself.

He shivered, seeing again the dawning horrified realisation on the dark faces as he picked up one of the captured AK47s. The tearing racket of the gun, and the screams of terror from the prisoners before life was blasted out of them.

It had shaken the squad though. They'd been a subdued bunch when, after watching the fort erupt in smoke and flame, he'd led them down the boulder strewn wadi, and back across the border.

There had been a quick handshake, and a quiet 'well done' from Colonel Prescott, plus the obligatory drink in the other ranks' mess that night.

And that's how it should have stayed, and would have stayed, if that damned reporter hadn't got young Jenkins drunk in that bar in Hereford. A good man, Cliff Jenkins. Pity he couldn't hold his liquor.

The big man rubbed his bearded jaw and smiled ruefully. Then everything had hit the fan. Colonel Prescott stalled manfully, but the media had scented blood and weren't about to let go.

The subsequent court martial had been a messy business. Jenkins had recanted his previous statement, while he and the squad had lied through their teeth. In the end he'd got away with a 'Not Guilty' verdict, although the press were almost vitriolic in their condemnation. However, his Army career was effectively over, and he'd resigned his commission immediately.

Unfortunately, certain sections of the media were far from finished and, having unearthed some of the tribesmen's families, were preparing a civil prosecution.

A career as a mercenary beckoned invitingly, but first there was the unfinished business of Cathie Farrel.

Catherine Ann Farrel. Even now, all these years later, he felt desire course through him when he thought of her. Tall, statuesque, blonde and intelligent, she was all he'd ever wanted in a woman.

A schoolteacher, with the added burden of an invalid mother, Cathie's life in a small village outside Hereford had been considerably restricted.

Their relationship had been curiously chaste. He'd suspected she was a virgin, and for that reason had never pressed her. There was a tacit understanding that, when he'd finished with the Army, they would marry. That was before the court martial. At their first meeting afterwards they'd quarrelled violently. In a fit of rage he'd admitted lying under oath. He remembered the look of contempt on her face as she turned away, and her parting shot. 'You're nothing but a cold-blooded killer!'

Then, their final tryst in Langley Woods, when he'd told her he was going away, and asked her to come with him. She'd refused angrily, saying that her mother was ill and couldn't be left. Furious, he'd grabbed her and she'd clung to him, weeping despairingly. What followed had been inevitable, he supposed. They'd made violent passionate love, there in the woods. When it was over she'd thrust him away, crying bitterly and saying she never wanted to see him again.

That had been their last meeting. A letter from an old Hereford acquaintance, received just as he'd completed his second contract in Angola, had mentioned Mrs Farrel's sudden death. A heart attack. She'd been ailing for years. It must have happened right after their break-up. Apparently Cathie had sold the house and moved to a teaching post in Swansea. Her family hailed from there originally.

It was just about then that he'd met up with an old friend and one time colleague, ex-SAS sergeant James Dumigan. He smiled sardonically at the memory. Jimmy Dumigan, alias James Duval, mercenary and arms dealer. That was Jimmy. Arms supplier to any crackpot organisation with a cause, and quite a few without!

Although not alike physically; Dumigan was stocky and barrel-chested, they shared certain similarities in temperament. Both loners, they had an equal aversion to rules and regulations. They'd never been close but, as Jimmy said, you didn't have to be bosom pals to make a profit!

Neither had managed to sustain a successful relationship with the opposite sex, but in Jimmy's view that was to be expected in their somewhat chancy profession. In his case this meant a missing wife and baby son. 'She just took off while I was away on a trip, John,' he'd said, growing maudlin during a marathon drinking session one evening. 'Never saw them again. No idea where they are. He'll be about twenty now, that boy, and I should have been there for him when he was growing up. Damn that woman. But I'll find him, John. Somewhere out there....' He'd fallen silent, staring vacantly into the distance.

And then that never to be forgotten day, when they'd contracted to supply arms to El Tigre and his Parador Liberation Front. Strange shook his head wonderingly. Fate plays some amazing tricks in life, but never more so than when our paths crossed with the PLF. The memories came flooding back....

Grenades, plastic explosive, limpet mines, Blowpipe missiles; plus automatic weapons with an ample supply of ammunition. Everything to sustain a guerrilla army, and small enough to be manhandled comfortably. Not a major shipment, but big enough.

They'd chartered a small steamer, the SS 'San Remo', out of Brownsville, Texas, for the run. Cash on delivery and no questions asked. 'Sanderson and Duval'. Suppliers of 'agricultural machinery', according to the bills of lading. That was Jimmy at his best. Cover your tracks. Always use an alias.

Sailing late at night, the 'San Remo' headed south across the Gulf of Mexico and through the Yucatan Channel at a steady eight knots. 'Not long now,' Captain Lopez, the swarthy skipper, said confidently. 'It is best to arrive in the evening.'

Jimmy had arranged it all. El Tigre and his guerrillas controlled the tiny port of Laduna, and that was where they would unload.

Cloaked in humid darkness, Lopez conned the rusty old steamer through the narrow harbour entrance. With only hand held torches to guide him, he eased his ship alongside the rickety wooden jetty. As shadowy figures materialised out of the gloom and seized the mooring ropes, the lean captain grinned triumphantly, teeth flashing white in the gloom. 'There you are, gentlemen. Delivery as promised.'

The guerrillas were waiting, with every form of transport imaginable. Jeeps held together with baling wire. Dodge trucks that had seen service in World War II, and so on, down to the humble pack mule. Eyes narrowed at the recollection, Strange remembered how smoothly everything had gone. Dawn had come hustling up, as it always did in the tropics; just as the last wheezing truck lumbered off the jetty.

'Senor Sanderson?' It was a strong voice, heavily accented and accustomed to command.

He turned slowly. Never appear anxious to meet a stranger, and anyway, he'd almost forgotten the alias. 'That's me.'

The man walking towards him was some five feet ten in height, of slim build, but with an aura of controlled power. There was arrogance and a hint of cruelty in the cold grey eyes. The patrician features, marred only by a small scar on the right cheek, indicated a dash of alien blood. Somewhere, far back, a conquistadore had stamped his genetic imprint on this man's ancestors.

'I am El Tigre. Come with me.' Again the imperious arrogance in the voice.

So this was the great El Tigre, otherwise El Liberatore, leader of the Parador Liberation Front. The natural successor, in the eyes of all liberation romanticists, to Che Guevara himself. The big man's hackles rose. Nobody talks to John Strange like that. Still...what the hell; he's the customer.

Together, they walked in silence along the crumbling jetty, until they reached the dilapidated warehouse at the end. A guard opened the door for them and stood aside.

Inside, clad in ragged green uniforms, the guerrillas, a mix of both sexes, were grouped around an open packing case, from which one them was struggling to remove a Blowpipe missile.

'Tell that stupid sod to be careful!' The words were out before he could stop them. Habit of command, he thought bitterly.

El Tigre's glance flicked sideways, then he barked an order. The man bending over the case straightened up and stepped back. His sullen gaze took in 'Sanderson', and dislike showed plainly on the heavy youthful features.

A wild one, big John thought wryly, noting the powerful build; the sudden flaring temper in the deep-set eyes. And with an understanding of English, I think. He realised the guerrilla leader was speaking again.

'You know this weapon?' The cold grey eyes surveyed him closely.

'Yes.' John said shortly.

'Good.' Then you can show us. I will interpret.'

The ex-SAS captain shrugged. 'Fair enough.' Shouldering his way through the group he was aware of their hostility. Nobody likes arms dealers, not even our customers.

The powerfully built young guerrilla moved aside reluctantly, dislike obvious in his sullen stare. Beside him, a tall, raven-haired, well-built young woman, a bandolier slung across her magnificent breasts, paused in the act of leafing through the missile handbook and surveyed 'Sanderson' coldly.

John, nobody can make enemies like you!

Stooping, he carefully withdrew the aimer from the box. 'Listen up.' His voice assumed its instructor's timbre. 'This is the aiming mechanism of the Blowpipe shoulder launched missile. And this,' he extracted a long grey tube, 'contains the missile. You assemble them…so.' Hands moving with practised ease, the big man clipped the two items together. 'Length just over fifty-five inches. Diameter three inches.' He cradled the complete weapon in his giant hands. 'Launch weight, twenty-four and a half pounds. Range….'

The guard called urgently from the doorway. There was the sudden bellowing roar of a low-lying plane, interspersed with the rattle of machine gun fire and the heavier crack of twenty millimetre cannon. The sounds faded quickly into the distance.

El Tigre snapped out orders and the guerrillas poured through the doorway and disappeared among the dilapidated buildings of Laduna.

'He will return,' the guerrilla leader said calmly, watching his followers take cover. 'He always does.' His eyes gleamed coldly. 'Bring the weapon. We may surprise him.' With 'Sanderson' at his heels he jogged across the dusty rutted roadway.

Cool bugger, the ex-captain thought admiringly. A faint drone intruded into his thoughts. That plane's out there on the seaward side of the town. My guess is he'll come in from the east. He swept the area with a practised eye. There! That pile of timber, just off the jetty. It'll be the 'San Remo' next time. Crouching behind the stack of wood, he lined up the aimer on the harbour entrance and sighted carefully. Waiting tensely, he was aware of the guerrilla chief kneeling beside him.

The sound of the circling plane intensified. 'Sanderson' tightened his grip on the aimer just as a Pucara ground attack aircraft burst out of the seaward bank of haze.

No worries about IFF! He squeezed the trigger and the missile wooshed out of the launcher. Coldly, using the CLOS thumb control guidance unit, 'Sanderson' watched the black speck impact against the nose of the oncoming plane.

The explosion threw the Pucara off course and it screamed away in a long shallow descent, before crashing among the trees on the far side of the bay. A column of flame erupted from the undergrowth.

There was a wave of cheering from the watching guerrillas. Rising to his feet, 'Sanderson' found El Tigre regarding him thoughtfully. Unclipping the empty tube, the big man tossed it into the water.

'You did well.' There was respect in the cold eyes...and something more. A calculating assessment. 'That plane has troubled us many times.'

'You're not out of the wood yet,' John said sharply. 'If he got a message off there'll be others. Even if he didn't, they'll still come looking for him.' He watched his partner hurrying down the gangway. 'Time we were moving, I think.'

'You alright, John?' 'Duval' eyed the big man curiously. 'Didn't reckon on you taking a hand.'

'Sanderson' shrugged. 'Somebody shoots at me I shoot back.' he said tersely. 'Anyway I thought El Tigre was entitled to a demonstration.'

The guerrilla leader's white teeth flashed in a smile. 'It was most impressive. I could use someone like you.'

'No doubt.' The ex-SAS captain felt vaguely uneasy. 'Unfortunately, we have to go. Time is money; and there is also the small matter of the Parador Air Force. Captain Lopez will want to be long gone before they appear. Let's get moving, Jimmy.' Already the screws were beginning to revolve, while a group of deckhands prepared to ship the gangway.

'A pity. I had hoped you would be co-operative. Now, I regret I must insist.'

Something in El Tigre's voice alerted the ex-captain. Turning sharply he found himself staring into the muzzle of a .44 calibre revolver.

'This is the thanks I get,' the big man said coldly, while his trained eye assessed the weapon. A Ruger Redhawk! One round from that would be enough.

'A thousand pardons,' Senor Sanderson. Raise your hands. You too, Senor Duval.' The Ruger menaced them both. El Tigre lifted his voice in a shouted command. A man and woman detached themselves from the waiting guerrillas and ran towards them. The woman carried a small black attaché case which she handed to her leader.

'Senor Duval, you, and you only, may lower your arms. Take the case. It contains the remainder of your money. I suggest you get aboard the ship now. As Senor Sanderson said, there may not be much time before the planes come.'

'What about....'

'Senor Sanderson stays.' There was a cold finality in the tone.

'Duval' eyed his partner unhappily. 'John....'

'Forget it. We haven't got time for long farewells.' As if to underline his remark the ship hooted impatiently. 'Once I've trained some of their guys I'm sure El Tigre will see reason. Bank my share.'

'Well....' Clutching the case, Jimmy ran up the gangway. It was immediately hoisted inboard, while the guerrillas cast off the mooring ropes.

John 'Sanderson' watched the 'San Remo' sidle away from the jetty. Carefully, Captain Lopez manoeuvred her out into the deep water channel. The water under the ship's counter frothed as she picked up speed. A last mournful toot of the foghorn and the steamer began to forge ahead.

'Again, my apologies, senor.' El Tigre replaced the Ruger in its holster. 'As I said, you are too valuable to let go. Now, let me introduce you to your new colleagues.' He indicated the young, heavily built guerrilla. 'Miguel Ramos, my second-in-command.' Ramos scowled. It was obvious that the comment about his handling of the missile still rankled.

Time to mend a few fences. 'Sorry about my remark earlier,' John said easily. 'Force of habit, I guess.' He held out his hand.

Ramos ignored the conciliatory gesture. 'A habit you would do well to control,' he said bitingly.

'Sanderson' grinned. 'I'll try to remember.'

'And this is Donna Estevan.' El Tigre waved a proprietary hand towards the sultry beauty whom John had last seen studying the Blowpipe manual. 'She leads the Sisters of the Revolution.'

'Sanderson' bowed. 'If all the sisters are like Senorita Estevan then I look forward to meeting them!'

The tall girl stared at him. 'I do not like arms dealers,' she said coldly. 'At best they are a necessary evil.'

El Tigre intervened, the ghost of a smile twitching his lips. 'Senor Sanderson has already demonstrated his worth. Now we must show him the delights of Parador.'

John grinned. In spite of everything, he already had a sneaking regard for this man. 'How could I refuse such an invitation. Lead on.'

The small ragged force was well into the hinterland and climbing steadily, when the planes appeared. High on the wooded ridge trail, 'Sanderson' watched the three oncoming aircraft as the guerrillas took cover. Magisters, he thought grimly. No wonder El Tigre's boys have been finding it tough going. The planes curved down towards the harbour in a long shallow dive.

'They are not troubling us this time.' He turned to find El Tigre at his side.

John nodded. 'My guess is the guy I downed got a message off. If I'm right they'll start searching out to sea. Look there!'

Even as they watched, the formation broke up. One plane banked away north along the coast; the second turned south; while the third headed seaward.

'Sanderson' scowled. 'They'll comb the area until they find the 'San Remo'. I'd say they're carrying bombs.' He shook his head regretfully.

El Tigre gave him a sidelong glance. 'The fortunes of war, my friend.' He signalled to Ramos and the convoy moved off.

Ten minutes later, still climbing, they heard the muted explosions. The big man grimaced wryly. Adios 'San Remo'. Looking back, he saw the column of black smoke beginning to tower above the horizon.

El Tigre eyed him sardonically. 'I think you are better here.' The distant thud of cannon fire came faintly down the wind. 'There will be no survivors.'

'Sanderson' nodded. 'Seems like it. Anyway, it gives me a reason to fight now.' They moved off in silence.

And that was how it had all begun. His Excellency smiled grimly at the memory. With the constant threat of a bullet in the head, there wasn't very much you could do about it. He had fought alongside El Tigre and his fanatical followers for almost two years. The big gringo's knowledge of weaponry and tactics had been a vital factor in their success, and the guerrilla leader knew it. Whether it was laying mines, setting up an ambush, repairing automatic weapons, or training recruits, ex-SAS captain John Strange, alias 'Sanderson', had done it all. He was the complete soldier.

At the same time he rode his luck, and his luck held. In the fiercest action he seemed to bear a charmed life. This did not go unnoticed. Gradually, El Tigre came to rely on him more and more. Ramos, on the other hand, hated the big man with a sullen hatred. He knew that 'Sanderson' had taken his place in the organisation and this was unforgivable.

The reaction of Donna Estevan, El Tigre's fiery mistress, and a guerrilla fighter par excellence, was more complex. John knew that, in the beginning, she had distrusted him. However, as time passed and his contribution to the cause grew, that distrust changed to a grudging admiration. It was when she began to find excuses to be alone with him, that the ex-SAS man realised he had a problem on his hands.

As for the rank and file, a sullen initial acceptance had changed during the campaign to what was virtually hero worship. This had finally been cemented by his daring rescue of the teenager, D'Inzencio. Left behind after a patrol, led by Ramos, had been ambushed; wounded and unable to walk, the youngster had been in desperate straits. Alone, 'Sanderson' had ghosted through the enemy lines, picked up the wounded boy, and carried him to safety through a hail of lead. That single act had elevated him to a place alongside El Tigre in the folklore of the revolution.

'Sanderson' knew this. He also suspected that a successful conclusion to the fighting would see his days numbered. No dictator risks someone stealing his men's loyalty. Furthermore, the problem of Donna Estevan wasn't going to go away.

So he was living on borrowed time. But, a fatalist by nature, he kept telling himself that something would turn up.

And something duly did. The Liberation Front fought their way across Parador and into San Miguel, the capital of the tiny state. Borne on a wave of wild enthusiasm, the ragged army swept across the plaza and through the gates of the presidential palace.

The elite Presidential Guards put up a fanatical resistance, dying to a man and inflicting heavy casualties on their attackers. Spraying bullets from his Kalashnikov, and with 'Sanderson' at his heels, El Tigre blasted his way into the presidential suite. Crouched behind his desk. El Presidente, Excellency Jamie Batiste, fired as the guerrilla leader charged through the doorway. El Tigre took a 9mm slug squarely in his forehead and died instantly, falling lifeless on the thick carpet. Flattened against the corridor wall, John 'Sanderson' plucked a grenade from his belt and, stretching forward, rolled it through the open doorway.

In the confined space the explosion reverberated like a thunderclap, and a blast of smoke and flame billowed out of the wrecked room. Cautiously, the big man inched forward and peered in. Batiste was sprawled across his desk, ripped apart by the grenade. Blood ran down the polished wood and dripped onto the carpet.

'Sanderson' eyed the tableau. The dead guerrilla leader spread-eagled in the doorway, and the equally dead dictator slumped across the desk.

Feet pounded down the corridor and he turned quickly, the AK47 menacing the guerrillas running towards him.

'El Tigre?' Shocked disbelief showed on all their faces.

'Sanderson' crossed himself. 'El Tigre is dead. He fell in the moment of victory. Where are Donna Estevan and Ramos?'

'They died crossing the plaza.' The speaker hesitated, then went on. 'There is no one left to lead us but you. Senor John, will you lead us?'

'Sanderson' looked at them, a band of ragged villainous looking figures, festooned with weapons and bandoliers of ammunition. A sudden wild hope flared in his mind. Here was a chance to live his life again. A chance to atone for some of the terrible things he had done.

'Very well.' He issued a string of rapid orders and the guerrillas hurried to do his bidding.

That had been twenty years ago, and now his dream of a small but prosperous country was a reality.

It had not been achieved easily, but then, he mused, nothing worthwhile ever is. The deceased Batiste had friends in neighbouring countries, men of influence, who were prepared to shelter and train dissidents. Those same dissidents were always probing Parador's frontier defences.

He'd seen the danger early. A special force had been created, their training based on SAS methods and vetted by himself. The Green Shadows were elite troops and they idolised their giant leader. Within a year the attacks ceased. Next, he'd initiated treaties of mutual co-operation with his neighbours, and that had finally eliminated the problem.

Agriculture was modernised, light industries were set up, and education was gradually made available for everyone. Corruption, which had been endemic in government departments, was rooted out ruthlessly. Laws were passed outlawing gun running, prostitution, and the possession of drugs. Each suspect was given a fair trial; he'd insisted on that, but the penalty, if found guilty, was always the same. Death, without appeal.

Draconian as these measures were, they had proved extremely effective. Gunrunning and drug smuggling dwindled and eventually petered out. Prostitution became a thing of the past. Better education, a higher standard of living and an improvement in morality saw to that. In fact, he'd been on the point of rescinding these extreme penalties when this latest case had surfaced.

John Davies, he mused. A good Welsh name. From Newport, Monmouthshire. Age twenty-two. He shook his head regretfully. Why would a young man, with everything to live for, take such a chance. No, I was right. There can be no exceptions.

He checked his watch. The execution should have taken place by now. Ramon would report back, once he'd made the statement to the press.

The harsh lines on his strong features softened as he thought of Ramon. When he succeeds me, God willing, that will set the seal on my plans. Parador, ruled by a native Paradorian. Rising, he walked across the room and switched on the TV set in the corner.

'…with deep regret,'…a picture of Ramon, standing in front of the assembled media, materialised on the screen,…'that El Presidente endorsed this sentence, but the welfare of the people of Parador is always paramount in his decisions.'

He watched as Ramon folded the paper and prepared to field questions. Shrugging massive shoulders, El Presidente switched off the set and, crossing to the window, stared down at the plaza below. The magnificent statue of El Tigre, flanked by smaller figures of Miguel Ramos and Donna Estevan, caught his eye. He smiled. How ironic that I, John Strange, the reluctant revolutionary, should be the only rebel leader left. Well, some day history would judge him, but he was satisfied that he had done his best. Parador was stable and prosperous. Still musing, he seated himself at his desk.

An hour passed. He was studying the last of the day's papers when there was a discreet knock on the door.

'Enter.'

The immaculate colonel padded noiselessly across the thick carpet, and came smartly to attention in front of the desk.

El Presidente looked up from the document he was reading and returned the colonel's salute. 'At ease, Ramon.' He motioned towards a vacant chair.' Everything has been taken care of?'

'Yes, Excellency.' D'Incenzio seated himself gratefully. It had been a long day. 'The young man acquitted himself well. He refused the blindfold. The media, of course, made their usual accusations.'

'Mm.' His Excellency reflected for a moment. 'We knew very little about him, other than the fact that his parents were dead.'

'Yes….' D'Incenzio coughed nervously and consulted a piece of paper he'd been holding. 'Though he did reveal to the priest that he had been brought up by a stepfather. It seems his natural father disappeared before the boy was born.'

El Presidente frowned. 'So what brought him to Parador?'

'Apparently there were rumours that the father was lost at sea, somewhere in this area.'

'Here?' El Presidente's interest sharpened. 'Did he know his name?'

'No. His mother would not tell him. It seems she never forgave the man for deserting her.'

El Presidente sighed. 'I can believe that. Some men…' His words trailed off. '…Anything else?'

'Yes, Excellency.' The colonel handed over a badly creased, sealed envelope. 'Commandante Hernandez asked me to give you this. It was found in the lining of the young man's jacket.' He hurried on, noting the sudden coldness in the piercing stare. 'Regrettably, it was not discovered when he was first arrested. Commandante Hernandez has disciplined the men in question.'

De Liberio's expression hardened. 'And the Commandante?' he inquired sharply.

D'Incenzio shifted uneasily in his seat.' He wishes to apologise to you personally.'

'I will see him tomorrow. Thank you, Ramon, that will be all.'

'Yes, Excellency.' On the point of leaving, D'Incenzio paused suddenly. 'There was something else. The young man said that his father had, at one time, served in the British Army. Goodnight, Excellency.'

'Goodnight.' The response was automatic as El Presidente grappled with the implications of the colonel's last remark. God help me, Jimmy; what have I done? The pain surfaced again, but he ignored it.

Reaching for the ornate silver paperknife, a gift from his beloved Green Shadows, De Liberio slit open the sealed envelope. For a long moment he stared into space, then, almost reluctantly, he extracted a small photo and a folded yellowing document. Surprise was etched sharply on the bearded features as he stared at the snapshot. The pain above his right eye intensified.

Slowly, El Presidente unfolded the heavily creased paper and smoothed it out. As he scrutinised it tensely, horrified realisation dawned on him. It couldn't be…. Pain, blinding all-encompassing pain, seared through his brain, and Juan de Liberio, President of Parador, slumped forward across his desk.

'And so, my friends, it is with a heavy heart that I take up the burden which El Presidente carried for so long. Goodnight and God be with you.'

'You reckon his story's kosher?' The tall saturnine reporter nodded towards the now blank screen. 'A brain haemorrhage?'

Ben Johnson, the night editor, shrugged. 'Who knows…but my bet is, yes. The whole country idolised de Liberio, and that guy was his protégé. It was always understood that he would take over when the president stepped down.'

Frank Magellan, international newsman, frowned thoughtfully. 'Not much known about de Liberio before he became president, is there?'

'That's true. He was the only leader still standing when the smoke and dust of the revolution cleared away. There were rumours that he was an English mercenary, but with that beard, and the shades he always wore in public…who knows. Ah, what the hell. File your story and let's go put the paper to bed.'

Acting President D'Incenzio relaxed in the big chair. The television crew had gone and he was alone.

De Liberio had been right. It was an awesome responsibility. Certainly the country was with him. El Presidente had always designated him as his successor. Naturally there would be those who would see this as a golden opportunity to create trouble, but they could be dealt with. The Presidente had made this a good country to live in and he would keep it that way.

Now, there was one last task to perform for his hero. Drawing the folded paper and the photo from an inside pocket, D'Incenzio laid them on the desk. Studying the picture closely, he nodded. There was no doubt. Younger certainly, but undeniably the same man. It explained much. How fortunate that he had been the one to find El Presidente. Placing the photo in the huge ornamental ashtray, the colonel unfolded the faded paper and scrutinised it carefully once again. Picking up a pen, he deleted a word and inserted an entry immediately below it. Tearing the document into several pieces he placed these also in the ashtray and, using his lighter, set fire to the pile. Grim-faced, Ramon D'Incenzio watched the glowing line traverse the torn document. It moved on inexorably, destroying everything in its path. A piece of paper curled with the heat, and the words 'Birth Certificate' caught his eye. The flame crept on and, under 'Mother', the name 'Catherine Ann Farrel, Schoolteacher', showed briefly.

Almost spent now, the glowing line crept towards the end of the paper. Under 'Father', he saw again where he'd deleted 'Unknown' and, below the deletion, in his own neat handwriting, the words; 'Juan de Liberio, President of Parador.'

The Fall and Rise of Walter's World

By William Clinkenbeard

In the dismal light of a late September afternoon, Walter studied the patchwork world before him with increasing anxiety. The sinking feeling in the pit of his stomach had returned, but this time it was more pronounced. The world he so enjoyed seemed to be disintegrating before his very eyes. There had been several intimations of its demise before, and each time he had been thrown into a micro-panic. You could be going along quite nicely, enjoying yourself without a care in the world and then suddenly....

He'd been having a good day up to now, following the usual pattern of working that he had established some time ago. It was familiar and comfortable. To begin the day he would always take at look at the paper first, usually the *Telegraph* but sometimes the *Times*. He didn't spend much time on the headline stories because he'd already seen most of them on the television news. But he liked reading the curious little titbits about celebrities, and he enjoyed doing the quizzes to determine your IQ. He read the financial section very carefully and kept up to date with business news. He selected one or two of the editorials to peruse and also spent time on the obituaries. After looking at the paper he liked to pop into the bank. It was, he thought, a good idea to keep an eye on your current account every day; just to make sure that it wasn't sliding into overdraft territory. Of all people, he ought to be able to manage that. Then he usually went into the building society to check on the amount of interest that was accumulating in their savings account. It had a bearing on their holiday planning. Next it might be the DIY warehouse or the wine store to see if there were any bargains going. Just last week he had seen a petrol lawnmower offered at an amazing price. He hadn't gone on to buy it of course, but it was certainly a bargain. The next stop was usually the holiday shop. He liked to study the pages offering luxurious resorts planted on stunning beaches in the Caribbean or the Indian Ocean, especially on the kind of gloomy day like today. Finally, he usually wandered around the supermarket to ensure he wasn't missing out on any specials. This was for Walter the usual morning routine. It had become essential for him, these forays into this world, and he always felt a little disorientated unless he did it.

But now this world was collapsing round him—not all at once, nothing dramatic, just strand-by-strand. The problem was the memory. He kept trying to reassure himself that it wasn't really *his* memory; it was the sheer number of secrets he needed to recall. It was like the Farside cartoon on the card he bought once to give to Muriel on her birthday. She'd been having a demanding time working in the bank, coming home battered and exhausted. Too many demanding customers and too few staff. The card pictured a classroom with students at their desks watching a lecturer standing at the blackboard. A student holding his hand in the air is seen to say in the bubble: 'Please sir, may I go home? My brain is full.'

That was Walter's problem. It wasn't *his* memory; it was simply that his brain was full. He had too many usernames and passwords to remember in order to access the web world he so much enjoyed. He simply could not recall all of them. Early on, when he was just beginning to get the hang of going online, it was made clear to him that you had to keep your password secret. *Never reveal your password to anyone.* This sound advice had been drilled into him ever since. He was being repeatedly warned, 'We will never ask you for your password.' Fair enough, but you couldn't operate just one password to access all your sites. If anyone did discover your sole password, they could access everything in your world: disaster! So he needed multiple passwords, and the larger his web world became, the more passwords he created, and the more passwords he created the more trouble he had in recalling them. On several occasions recently he had been informed by the bank or the building society that he was being denied access because he had entered an incorrect password. Then he had to waste more time getting a new one. He had spent so much time in Help! that it cut down his time in his web world. He hated getting lost in Help! It was even getting to the point where he was being denied access to sites where secrecy surely didn't matter. After all, who would really care about his meanderings in the 5 PM. Restaurant Guide site? Was this an MI5 matter? Walter soon learned to stop trying after only two password attempts. It was that third time wrong that got you: three strikes and you're out. Web baseball. But this reluctance to go for a third try led only to putting off the problem. He just wasn't getting into some of the sites he loved and so became more and more fearful of ever trying again. It wasn't something he could talk about to everyone, for it seemed trivial. How could you admit to people that you had forgotten your password to Virgin Wines? But to Walter it was anything but trivial, and now panic was silently creeping, step-by-step, its way into his heart.

Being a logical person, he kept thinking about a logical solution. One answer might have been to list all his usernames and passwords on paper. But to keep the list secure he would then need to lock it away somewhere, perhaps even in the safe. But if he did that he would need to remember the combination of the safe, and if he forgot that he really would be in trouble. Moreover, wouldn't it be stupid to have to go to the safe each time you wanted to go online? He thought about storing his list on the pc's memory—making a special site with his usernames and passwords. But then if anyone found that file, it would give them even easier access to the whole shebang. Walter didn't know what to do. Every time he applied his mind to the problem he started to break out in a cold sweat.

Since retiring from the accountancy firm, Walter liked returning to his desk, the desk with the polished top supporting the flat screen, under which the keyboard slid out so effortlessly. He didn't miss the work, the endless going over of figures. But he did miss the discipline of sitting down to do *something*. So there was, he thought, something about coming into the study, sitting down in his leather executive chair, and switching on the pc to enter an alternative world. When he signed on and got to the *Welcome, Walter!* page he always felt a surge of adrenalin. There were moving adverts and colourful photos and a variety of different departments to check out. He couldn't explain it to people, but each possibility seemed like it was an open door to a new, vast, and intriguing world. He could get the latest celebrity gossip, try for the holiday of a lifetime, meet a stranger in the chat room, discover a better savings account, or check out the weather for tomorrow. He could view the pictures transmitted by a web camera sited on some distant sunny beach. His long list of favourite places was meticulously organized. Each time he double-clicked a site he felt that he was opening a door that allowed him into a space that was uniquely his. He was comfortable in this world. It didn't really make many demands on him, except for the irritating pop-ups that took up time and distracted his attention, although even they were sometimes interesting. In the various spaces he could move around freely and dream his way anywhere, into the great cities of the world or remote islands. No one pestered him for money, no one came to the door wanting him to buy double-glazing or new gutters or a conservatory. No one complained about their annual accounts or their bills or their wives. Everyone in the web was just so nice, so courteous, so undemanding. It was a great world.

But now this world seemed to be slipping away from him and he didn't know what to do. Muriel couldn't seem to help. She had never become computer-literate. She didn't really comprehend his problem and didn't seem all that bothered. She would stand for a minute or so at his side and watch unfeelingly at the screen. 'I don't know, Walter,' she would say without enthusiasm. 'Maybe it will come back to you. Anyway, I've got to go out now.' After she retired from the bank she took up helping in that bloody charity shop. She was now spending two or three days a week sorting through old clothes and was no help at all for Walter. He couldn't think of anyone else to ask for help.

It was that very afternoon that the crunch came, and that's when Walter began to unravel. There was some problem when he went to log off and shut down, a dialogue box that he couldn't understand. He had to turn off the pc manually, but not to worry. It would probably be OK in the morning. But in spite of himself, Walter spent most of the rest of the day worrying about it. The next morning, when he had plucked up enough courage to switch the machine on, it happened. This was what he had dreaded. When Walter tried to get into his server, it asked for his password. He hadn't used that password for…well…for months, perhaps even several years. He made several tries, but nothing worked. He was shut out, completely denied. His very lifeblood, everything he enjoyed, was cut off. Walter sat at the keyboard, absolutely helpless. His world was gone, the world of the news, the bank, the building society, the world of books and tools and wine, the endless spaces where you could wander at will and look and meditate, where no one harangued you, and where you felt at home.

Walter was paralysed, unable to set about getting back online. He could, he thought, probably manage it by getting outside help, but just getting back online this time wasn't going to solve the enduring secrecy problem. It was always going to be there. For the rest of the morning he moped around the house, trying to get involved in this or that. It didn't work. Everything seemed drained of meaning.

Finally, in the afternoon, which happened to be a Sunday afternoon, Walter went outside in desperation. It was a sunny day. His next-door neighbour was washing the car and shouted a greeting over to him. The trees in the surrounding gardens were magnificent in their autumn colours, burnished bronze, red and yellow. The water in the Firth of Forth was calm and reflected the deep blue sky. Walter strolled down the footpath, meeting people who smiled and nodded. He stood up straighter, taking more notice of what was happening around him. He almost felt good…. well, almost. But something was bothering him, niggling away at him. It was like the curious feeling you get when you have forgotten or neglected something. He put his hand to his back pocket, but his wallet was there. He touched his front pocket, but the door key was there. He shrugged, as if to cast off the feeling, but it endured. What was it exactly that was missing? He stopped at the top of the steps leading down to the park and grasped the railing decisively as if it would help him find the missing piece. Below him, children were playing football in the park, running and shouting for the ball. A couple were flying a kite, and it dived and ducked on the command from each hand. An old man was throwing a tennis ball for his black lab, who chased it at full speed and retrieved it in joyful triumph. The light and colour and sound and movement were slightly bewildering to Walter as he stood, holding onto the rail and watching. But what kept niggling away at him? It was something to do with…. with what exactly? Something to do with *permission*. Yes, that was it—permission. And then it dawned on him, as he stood on the path, overlooking the patchwork park with the sun on his back: in this world he had needed no username and no password. He had just entered it, freely.

978-0-595-40340-0
0-595-40340-9

Printed in the United Kingdom
by Lightning Source UK Ltd.
113452UKS00001B/127-327